JOURNEYS

JOURNEYS

Diane Brenda Bryan

To order additional copies of this book, contact:
Xlibris Corporation
1-888-795-4274
www.Xlibris.com
Orders@Xlibris.com
20249

In Loving Memory of a Remarkable Man
My Soulmate: JACK MURPHY

FOR
All our children and
the grandkids

THANKS TO:

Dori Popenoe, for the lovely cover art.
My colleagues at the Boca Raton Writers' Roundtable,
for their support and, especially, to Mark Jacoby
and David Shapiro for their relentless criticism and comfort.
Boca Raton S.W. Regional Library for the use of the room.
Civil War Archives

CHAPTER I

"'T IS A CURSE, a curse, fer sure." The woman spat at the ground as she jabbed the toe of her worn shoe into the hard, unrelenting earth. She raised her right hand, cupping it over her eyes and scanned the little field before her. There they be, her husband and son. The poor darlin's, laborin' and strainin' ta harvest enough potatoes ta feed them and, the Good Lord willin', enough ta sell fer a few coins. "Och," she sighed. Even if they could grow some more, they would jist be destroyed by the wet summer when it came, she reflected. The terrible dampness brought the blight fungus that turned potatoes rotten.

Maureen McCullough was a tall, beautiful woman whose fair attributes were almost hidden by the desperate conditions of her life—the deprivation to which she and her family were exposed. A once lovely body was undernourished and almost frail. Soft, cornflower blue eyes had become as hard as steel from the desolation upon which they looked; beautiful blonde hair was pulled back and covered with a knotted cloth. "Rags," she would say. "We are beggars in rags." Yet, Maureen maintained an inner strength that enabled her to wake up and face each day.

She stood quietly for a moment, gazing across the field at her loved ones, then she called out, "Eamon, Sean, come have a bite ta eat and some milk. You will be wearing yourselves out, I fear."

They looked up and waved. "We will be along in a bit, wife," Eamon called back. He raised his basket, showing it almost half-filled with potatoes.

The poor dears, she thought, diggin' and scratchin' like hungry animals—and we are that fer sure. Nothin' but failed crops. Oh, Jaysus, we will all die in this Great Starvation?"

She remembered the stories she heard of the quarter million that died in the famine of 1741. And here it is, a hundred years later, she thought, and we are still dyin'! Four years of blight and crop failure and things still worsenin'. "'Tis Black '47 fer sure," she muttered. Maureen knew that if they continued unable to meet the rent for this sad piece of earth, they would be evicted. So far, luckily, their landlord had shown compassion and they were allowed to remain in their crumbling cottage. But for how much longer? She inhaled sharply.

Eamon, a tall, sturdy man in his youth, had whittled away to a lean, sparse figure but remained stubbornly strong and still handsome. His eight-year old son Sean had the same physical attributes of his father.

A little later, they entered the ramshackle house with a basket of "lumpers". Maureen immediately set them to cook in the worn out boiling pot. "Fer sure, these are the poorest grade the ground could give up."

Eamon said, "Too bad we do not have a pig and some oats so we could give somethin' to the landlord fer the rent."

"Niver you mind the landlord, with us not havin' enough barely ta breathe life," she retorted. "Go fetch a bowl of salt water and let us 'dip at the stool'."

As soon as the "praties" were ready, the three of them sat around the three-legged stool upon which Eamon had placed the bowl of salt water.

Suddenly Maureen said, "I will be goin' into Tanniwilly tomorrow."

They knew what that meant and dreaded the thought. She would go into the city, as did many wives and daughters, to beg or perhaps get some food from the soup kitchen set up by the "bloody" British.

Eamon worried about the riots and violence in the streets. More and more, desperate people were breaking the law. Blushing with humiliation, he asked, "Darlin', do you not believe we can do fer now? At least, fer another few days? How I despise your goin' into that vipers' nest."

"Luv, I will be foine. I mind me own business and keep ta meself, you know that," she answered staunchly. "I will not be takin' part in any shenanigans. As soon as I can beg a few shillin's and buy some food, I will be comin' right back."

Sean offered, "Well, at least, Mam, let me go with you."

"Oh no, Son. Only women and little girls beg. You and your Da have enough ta do here. I will do jist foine, I tell you."

They knew better than to argue with her.

Maureen arose early in the morning. She wanted to prepare some boxty bread so her husband and son would have something to eat with their skimmed milk when they came in from the field later in the day. Poor dears, she thought, dependin' mainly on those cursed potatoes and whatever magic she could produce with the sorry things.

Conditions were deteriorating, and, more and more, she dreaded going into the city. An air of rebellion was everywhere. People were reduced to stealing, or worse, to keep alive. She bade her family goodbye with a valiant attempt at cheerfulness. "I will return soon, me luvs, perhaps with a foine chicken or two. Say a prayer to blessed St. Jude fer me." As she walked out the door, she turned once more, a strained smile on her lovely face. "The Good Lord smile upon you this day."

As she trudged along, she was reviled by the sight of dead bodies of peasants who had either starved to death or had succumbed to typhus, cholera, dysentery or scurvy and had fallen in the night, in the fields or by the roadside. "Oh, Jesus, Joseph and Mary!" she cried. "The rats will get fat, fer sure, devourin' the poor souls, and the dogs and cats will have a feast at the open trenches filled with uncoffined bodies. Lord save us," she prayed.

Maureen could smell the stench from Tanniwilly long before

she walked down the filthy, dilapidated streets. "Oh, Lord, be with me this day," she said aloud as she crossed herself. Walking along the broken, neglected cobblestones, she became uneasy at the sight of the unusually large crowds of beggars in torn, dirty rags. How desperate they look. This is a place of utter despair. A place to be feared. Her heart pounded as the crowd jostled her about. Instinct told her to flee but practicality and determination made her stay. "It will not be easy this day," she muttered. "I have niver seen so many beggars on the street."

Suddenly, Maureen spotted the greengrocer whom her family had known for years. She recalled that he had been most kind at times, helping them out with a bit of food. "Hello now, Mr. Byrnes, an' how are you this day?" She tried hard to smile. "An' your lovely wife and little ones, are they all grand?"

"Oh, Mrs. McCullough, sure an' 'tis a sight fer sore eyes, you are." Mr. Byrnes knew she had come to beg but he would not allow her to humble herself. He added quickly, "'Tis glad I am ta see you. I have somethin' for you and your men at home."

Maureen feigned reluctance but the good man insisted, "I have an extra fowl I would like you ta have. The wife an' I have been meanin' ta visit with you but toimes are so hard here, we are afraid ta leave." He pushed a clumsily wrapped chicken into her hands and turned away from the tears he saw glistening in her eyes. She placed the precious gift into the large, handmade shopping bag she carried and said, in a soft voice, "The Good Lord bless you."

He could see that she was embarrassed, so he continued to make conversation. "'Tis the worst disaster yet, I b'lieve. They are droppin' like flies all over the place."

Maureen grew anxious to leave with her prize. Already she envisioned the feast they would have. "You are a kind man and we are ever so grateful." She took his hands in hers and pressed them with a firmness that displayed her gratitude.

"Go on with you now. Go home. 'Tis no good fer a woman alone ta be on these streets. The Lord be with you." Mr. Byrnes hurried back to the remains of what had been his shop, now nothing more than a broken down shed.

Maureen hastened to the road that would take her home. She never noticed the two men watching her as she spoke with Mr. Byrnes.

*   *   *

They found her crumpled in a heap by the side of the road, about a kilometer out of Tanniwilly. Eamon and Sean had gone to look for her when she did not return at the expected time. They bent over her still figure. There was no sound, no movement.

"Oh, Jaysus, oh, Lord," Eamon kept repeating. "Help your humble servants." He rocked his wife in his arms as Sean, tears streaming down his drawn, colorless cheeks, cried. "Oh, Mam, speak to your lovin' husband and son. We love you and need you. Come now, Mam, open your lovely eyes."

As they lifted her, she suddenly whimpered. "Oh, thank the Lord," Eamon shouted. Sean kissed his mother on the cheek. "You are foinc, Luv," Eamon told her. "Do not fear. We are takin' you home."

Maureen's eyelids fluttered briefly, a faint smile of recognition and thankfulness on her face.

Home. Home to the stone cottage. They laid her down on the pile of hay in one corner of the damp, mud floor and covered her with one of their tattered blankets. Eamon lit a fire with a little bit of fagots. He placed the few potatoes they had salvaged that day into a pot of boiling water. Sean sat on a chair near his mother and gently patted her head and wiped her face with a cool, wet rag. "Oh, Sweet Jesus in heaven, help Mam get well," he whispered.

After they ate the meager repast of boiled potatoes and the hot liquid, they tried to awaken Maureen. Will you not have a bite ta eat, Luv?" She stirred briefly. Oh, the poor dear, he cried inwardly, so beaten up and bruised. I could kill the murderin' beasts!

She lifted her eyes to answer him, and her look reflected the deep love she felt. "Oh, Darlin', 'tis tired I am. Jist a bit of rest and I will be foine. Seein' you and Sean is all the medicine I need. Maybe a cup of potato broth will do me fer now." Within a few minutes after she sipped the weak liquid, she was asleep.

Sean said, "Well, Da, I think we will hafta wait fer Mam's story. What evil creatures did this? She niver did harm ta anyone. Poor Mam." He began to cry.

Eamon put his arms around his only child. "Come now, lad. We had best be gettin' a bit of the old shuteye ourselves. There is lots ta be done and Mam ta be looked after, too. Go say your prayers, with a special one ta St. Jude." Eamon kissed his son on the forehead. The boy went over to his crude bedstead and threw himself down on the pile of hay.

During the night, both father and son shed tears as they listened to Maureen cry out in her sleep. The anguish, the horror in her voice spoke of what she had suffered there alone on that road.

Eager for the details of what happened, they were both at her side when she awakened the next morning. She drank some water and ate a piece of the hardened boxty bread. "Eamon, I will tell you what happened but you must promise me you will do nothin' ta put yourself or the boy in peril. In these hard toimes, people have murder in their hearts." She silently vowed that he will never know who the brutes were for she would not describe them. He might have to pay too dearly for the revenge he would seek. In reality, she had not recognized her attackers. They had, no doubt, come in from Killybegs or Dunfanaghy or, for that matter, from anywhere in this godforsaken Donegal.

Slowly, she told her loved ones of her meeting with Mr. Byrnes, his gift of kindness, and how she decided to go home straight out because she had grown fearful of the crowds. "It was not until I was on the outskirts of the city that I noticed these two rundown, dirty lookin' fellows walkin' along near me. I could see they were eyein' the shoppin' bag and the fear gripped me. They wanted ta rob the fowl Mr. Byrnes gave me! I quickened me step but in me heart I knew I was in dire circumstances."

Eamon and Sean shifted uneasily in their seats. Maureen closed her eyes for a moment and then continued. "The two beggars kept gettin' closer to me until they were beside me. I looked at them, afraid to speak, grippin' the bag firmly and closer ta me. Then one of them says, 'Now, now, luv'ly lady, do not be afraid. We jist want that bag and we will have leave of ya.' Oh, Eamon, I did not know what ta do. I could not give up the bag, so I started ta run as fast as I could. But not fer long. The brutes were upon me in a minute's toime.

"'You stupid wench!' one shouted as he knocked me down to the ground while the other wrenched the bag from me hand. Oh, Sweet Jesus, I cried out. Do not kill me, I begged. At that, they both kicked me hard in the back and stomach. I thought I was a dead one, fer sure, there on that lonely roadside—food fer the rats. I cannot remember anythin' after that. 'Tis a strong blow they dealt me on the head." She began to whimper.

Eamon held her close. "Sh-h-h, all right, Luv. Stop your cryin'. You are here safe with us now." He felt a murderous rage well up and the urge to run out down the road to find the filthy beggars. His hands ached to circle their throats and throttle them. He controlled himself. It would be like looking for a needle in a stack of hay.

Sean brought his mother some water and a boiled potato. Maureen tried hard to eat but exhaustion overcame her and she begged them to let her sleep again. "I will have somethin' ta eat after I sleep a bit more. 'Tis weary I am from the terrible struggle and fear of it all."

Eamon motioned to his son. They said no more.

*   *   *

Several weeks passed before Maureen was sufficiently recovered to go about her usual chores. The stringent diet they were forced to rely upon was not conducive to a healthy state of mind and body. Eamon and Sean struggled on, with conditions worsening by the day. The phytophora infestations continued to ravage the potato fields, bringing nearly total failure that year.

One day, Eamon said to his wife, "Darlin', we will be starvin' ta death soon if we do not get some nourishment. I have been thinkin' about joinin' the road works program that the British have set up . . ."

Maureen interrupted, "Oh, no, Eamon. You must not. 'Tis known that too many have fallen and died by the wayside, too weak to work, too sick from the disease and the hunger. No, Eamon, I will not have you breakin' half a ton of stones every day—and dyin' fer it. No!"

Within a few months, it was a moot question. The road work program was abandoned, but there were soup kitchens set up which fed many; eventually they too were shut down.

As they sat eating their measly dinner one evening, Eamon commented, "Well, I was talkin' to Mr. Bailey and he tells me that the 1838 Irish Poor Law has been extended. The landlord will be responsible for relief of the poorest on the smallest properties. Now the 'bloody' British have set up workhouses. There is one right here in Ballyshannon and another in Carrick-on-Shannon in Leitrim, and many more, I suppose. You know, Luv, 'twill not be long before the landlord takes back the land and sends us off ta one of those places—us not bein' able ta pay the rent . . ."

"Oh, Lord, Eamon, will we hafta leave our home?"

He replied, ruefully, "Home, is it?" Seeing the look of desolation upon her face, he quickly added, "Darlin', that is what I have been told. What choice do we have? Give up the land or starve ta death. At least, in Ballyshannon, we will be fed oatmeal, milk and potatoes . . . as little as that might be."

Sean sat down next to him. "Da, is it true that families are separated in the workhouses? I do not want ta be apart from you an' Mam." He had tears in his eyes.

"Do not fret, boy. I will be close at hand; so will your mam. You are a big lad and I am sure they will put you ta work with me."

After several minutes of silence, a shout came from Maureen's lips. "No! I will die before I go with my loved ones ta the 'gaol', ta the grey walls of that hell. Eamon, we hafta find another way."

The years 1848 and 1849, saw another onslaught of fungus and, like others, the family suffered terribly as they struggled, constantly threatened with eviction, with starvation, and always with the specter of death before their eyes. The McCulloughs were rapidly sinking into an abyss of despair. They realized that eventually they would lose their home and their land. Little by little, their neighbors were evicted. Some were sent to the workhouses. Great numbers of them opted to give up the land and accept passage abroad. They knew the workhouses were centers of contagion—death houses. For the landlords, giving them passage abroad was a much cheaper solution than the workhouses. The hapless victims had hopes that going to a new land held some promise.

When the landlord's agent approached the McCulloughs with the news of their eviction, they were offered the alternative to the workhouse: the landlord would pay passage for the family if they wished to emigrate to Canada or America where, he assured them, "You will have a chance to work and make a decent life for yourselves. I am truly sorry for you. You are good people. But . . . 'tis that or the road to the poorhouse."

Eamon's first instinct was to retort with a resounding, "Kiss me arse!" but Maureen's voice cut him short. "Thank you kindly. We will talk it over. Would you be good enough ta come back in a day?"

The agent had always admired her, not only because beneath the grime and the hunger she was a beauty, but also for the courage and pride she displayed. In a soft voice, he replied, "Surely, I can do that." He tipped his hat and was gone.

The rest of that day and far into the night, the family debated what course to follow. After Sean fell asleep, Maureen said in a firm voice, "Now, husband, I will tell ya what we are ta do and I will hear no arguments to the contrary."

Eamon anticipated something like this. He knew his wife would not take a position in front of their son. She always wanted

Sean to believe that his father made decisions for the family. Taking her hand in his, he said lovingly, "So, dear wife, what are you thinkin'?"

"We have no choice, if we are ta survive, Eamon. Thousands have already left the homeland. 'Tis sad I feel that we must now do the same. We hafta think of Sean—more than ourselves."

"I will not fight you, my darlin'. Come now, let us ask St. Jude ta help us in our desperate hour."

They knelt. Neither was able to sleep that night.

CHAPTER II

WINTER 1853. THE wretched group stood solemnly by the roadside, watching as the thatched roofs of their cottages were torn down. Some of the homes were set on fire, as well. The McCulloughs were among the tenants who had agreed to emigrate. As the flames reduced the pitiful shacks to rubble, eyes welled with tears. Sean asked, "Why do they hafta destroy our homes? We are leavin' . . ."

"Son," Eamon explained, "they want ta make sure we will not change our minds, that there is nuthin' left ta go back ta. Anyway, the landlord will soon have the land sold ta the wealthy farmers who will be bringin' in their cattle and sheep."

"And, I am sure they will be buildin' decent places ta live in," added Maureen. "Nuthin' like the filthy, sorry pigpen we had to endure . . ." Her voice caught in her throat.

Eamon quickly placed his arm around her shoulder and shushed her. "We will not show the bastards weakness. The McCulloughs have always been proud. Sure an' we will not betray that pride now."

Around them, other evicted tenants were complaining. Eamon raised his voice. "C'mere, do you follow? Stop your keenin' 'Tis to America we are goin'. Are you not grateful fer the chance?"

Pain was clearly etched on their faces. Leaving the "auld sod" was not easy. Fierce loyalty to Ireland and the Catholic Church held them captive. Had not their priest always told them to resign themselves to God's will, to remain peaceful, to pay their rent? For this they had struggled through deprivation while thousands of bushels of corn and the best of the potatoes were taken from them as they stood, under British guard, and watched helplessly. These crops would be shipped to England and sold abroad while they were starving. Helpless then and helpless now, they watched their homes go up in smoke.

The landlord had arranged for two British ships to be at the ready at Donegall Quay where the evicted tenants would board either the one to Canada or the other to America. The McCulloughs had opted for America, to the City of New York, which they had heard was full of Irish and opportunity.

The commonality of the emigrants who gathered on the quay that day was their rags and the signs of hunger and disease. Maureen held her son close to her while Eamon tried to stand tall in the midst of the bedlam. Cries of anguish; supplications to Jesus.

The loading of passengers began. They were herded aboard the SPIRIT OF HOPE. Soon the ship was bursting with the poor, starving, vermin-ridden numbers who clung to their pathetic, ragged little bundles. The McCulloughs shuffled along, propelled by the pushing and shoving masses urged on by the guards. "Get along with you now. Hurry up. Keep movin'!"

As they filled in the dark, musty spaces between decks and in the hold, Maureen could not restrain herself. "Oh, Eamon, fer sure we are in purgatory. Look at the stacks of cots and the filth. We will be sleepin' worse than animals, without a breath of fresh air."

"Do not worry, Luv, we will be in a new land soon. Now we hafta be strong." Eamon noticed Sean's distress as he glanced about the murky, narrow spaces. "Come, lad, 'twill not be so bad. We will make it all right." Sean smiled weakly.

The first mate appeared, assigned them to their bunks and explained how food would be rationed out. They set sail and soon the brig rounded the promontory of Howath, taking the north channel, in a southerly wind. The north shore of Ireland was still in sight the following morning. Once they navigated the promontory of Donegal, the shoreline became indistinct. The ship headed out to the open sea.

In the days that followed, the oatmeal or biscuits and stale water barely kept the passengers alive. Even at that, the rations meted out were less than promised and, before long, the hunger and unsanitary conditions began to take their toll. Nights were filled with cries of pain and despair; the strangulated last gasps of the dying; the foul air; the uncontrollable body fluids and waste. Half-naked, starving, ill with dysentery and fever, many died.

When some members of the crew became ill, the captain approached the passengers. "How many of you brave lads are willin' to take their places. You will get additional rations and better sleeping quarters."

Eamon whispered to Maureen. "I will do it. I am strong."

Maureen whispered back. "Eamon, I am afraid fer us ta be apart, even fer a moment. Sean's head bobbed up and down in agreement.

"If we are ta survive, we must be brave. We must help ourselves as much as we can. This is a chance, some hope . . ." Eamon's voice trailed off.

His wife looked at him and then at their surroundings. The fetid atmosphere, breathed in day and night, made them sick— physically and spiritually. Perhaps this *was* an opportunity for them, an opportunity to save themselves. "All right, Eamon," she said reluctantly.

The captain picked the most able-bodied of the volunteers. Physically, Eamon had fared better than most. Although slimmed down, he was still quite strong. The captain put him in charge of a small group to maintain decks and galley and, with his earnest prompting to the master, Sean was given a job as cabin boy. The change afforded the family a space closer to the top deck and ever so often, at night, they would creep up to the stairwell to breathe in the salt air and marvel at the luminous appearance of the water. They delighted in watching the sea, crowded with large numbers of 'slobbs' of various sizes, forms and colors and the Portugese men-of-war as they positioned themselves in the breeze and rode the crest of the waves.

The improved rations plus the extra scraps Eamon gathered

from the galley greatly improved their situation. Sleeping in less cramped quarters made conditions a little more bearable.

One day, when Eamon was down in the hold with the first mate, preparing rations for distribution, he noticed a slight movement behind the sacks of oatmeal. The mate had seen it as well. They quickly removed several of the stacked sacks only to discover a man crouching in fear. When the stowaway was brought up on deck, the captain was livid. "Throw the wretch overboard!" he ordered.

Eamon quickly intervened. "Beggin' your pardon, Sir, would it not be a good idea ta put him ta work with the crew? We could use the help."

The captain reflected for a moment. "Fine. But he will not get a bit of rations. If any of you want to give the begger somethin', that is your choice. But, when we get to Cork Island, we will drop him off."

The poor creature thanked the captain over and over again for sparing his life. The captain rewarded him with a kick in the pants and the admonition, "Earn your way or you will taste the briny blue!"

In the weeks that followed, Eamon gave the grateful man as much food as he could salvage without depriving his own family. Illness and death had become a daily ritual and the passengers, with no medicine or proper care, lay in their berths praying for relief, many painfully aware that they would never see America. The burials at sea left the emigrants dispirited and deprived of hope; even the unseaworthy vessel in which they sailed gave them cause for alarm. On a daily basis, voices were raised in prayer. "Oh, sweet Jesus in heaven, take the souls of the departed to your bosom. Bless us and take away the pain. Bring us safely to a new land for the sake of our children. Bless your faithful servants, O Lord." Many yearned for the sight of one of their beloved priests and even though they had not one reason to be thankful, they clung to their unwavering faith.

The only relief from their "dungeons", for those who were not bedridden, was the occasional trip to the upper deck where they escaped the foul atmosphere below. Some days, when the climate permitted, they gathered around a crude fireplace to cook some salt meat, a special ration. Many of the passengers refrained from eating this meat because of the thirst it created. Their drinking water supply, inadequate at best, was even sparser because the captain shortchanged them by giving half-rations to the children, and, at times, even cheating the adults.

As they gathered around the fire, often a voice would be raised in song and then the others would join in to keep their spirits up. One blustery, wet day, within sight of Cork Island, the captain ordered two of his men, "Prepare to lower a boat. Get that miserable parasite and take him to yonder shore. He has enjoyed enough of our hospitality." He laughed raucously. The men fetched the poor soul who had nothing but scanty rags on his half-starved body. Eamon and the crew witnessed the scene. Just before the rowboat reached the island, the stowaway was cast out into the freezing water. They all watched as he struggled against the tide to reach the shore where he stood, frightened and shivering, but lucky to be alive. Eamon lifted a hand in farewell. The forlorn, deserted creature raised a hand in return.

CHAPTER III

THE VOYAGE EVERYONE anticipated would take three weeks took more than three months. The vicious winds and freezing cold of the North Sea forced the ship to pull into island harbors along the way. Seasickness added to the plight of the unhappy travelers.

Finally, the Spirit of Hope arrived at the Port of New York on May 15, 1849, with a little more than half of its original human cargo of 238, the dead having been buried at sea. As the ship slipped into its berth, the tattered, pathetic passengers crowded the decks to get a glimpse of the place they had heard referred to as "heaven's front parlor". Thankfully, the weather was good. The first view revealed Staten Island, a heavily wooded area, and the spire of Trinity Episcopal Church. Silent at first, they suddenly raised their voices to such a din that the master of the ship threatened, "Quiet! or I'll throw you into the harbor."

Eamon held Maureen close as she gripped Sean's hand. "Well, Luv, we made it. 'Tis a new life for us now. We will get our landin' money and with the few pounds, we will find us a place ta live."

As the sick and weary emerged from the ship, they were herded together on the wharf. The captain advised, "You will make your own way now. New York is a big city where there's work to be found and an opportunity to start a new life. I'll be takin' my leave now." He paused. "God bless you all."

Suddenly, voices were raised in protest. "Where are we ta go?" "What are we ta do?" The captain shouted above them, "Go on with you or you'll go back the way you came!" The thought of returning to the horrors of the ship was a sobering one. The crowd fell silent.

Only Eamon found his voice. "Master O'Hara, where do we go ta pick up our landin' money?"

O'Hara and his crew exchanged knowing looks. "Landin' money, is it? What fairy tale have you been listenin' to?"

"Beggin' your pardon, Sir, but we were told by the land agent, Mr. Bailey, that the English Emigration Commissioners ordered the landlords ta provide at least one pound of landin' money, upon arrival, for each tenant." Eamon felt a hard knot forming in the pit of his stomach.

"I never heard of any such money ever bein' sent or received by anyone. 'Tis a fool's tale. Now, get on with you." Then, softening his tone, "And may the Good Lord keep you from harm." The captain made the sign of the cross and turned to go on board.

As fear and uncertainty gripped them again, their voices slowly rose in measured tones, but a flash from the captain's eyes as he turned from the gangplank subdued the protestors. "The poor bastards," O'Hara muttered. "It's no 'golden door' they'll be passin' through."

There they stood: abandoned and stranded on the tip of the island called Manhattan. Within a few minutes, as if unleashed by some magical signal, a group of men and boys began to circulate amongst the emigrants. With promises of finding them lodgings, they grabbed belongings and took from the unsuspecting travelers whatever few coins they possessed. Those who resisted immediately fell victim to these predators who were nothing more than thugs and thieves.

The McCulloughs clung fast to their possessions and rejected offers from the culprits. Eamon walked over to help an old woman as she argued with a youth who was insisting on taking her bag. As he wrested the bag from the boy's hand, he heard Maureen scream his name. Turning quickly, he saw that she was struggling with a brute of a man who Sean was pummeling with his fists. Eamon rushed to them. Pulling the man aside, he slammed his fist into his face. "Ya dirty thief, get away from us!" The man ran off.

Eamon was wise to the way of "street people". He had seen too many hustlers in Tanniwilly.

Maureen said, "Do ya think maybe some of them are really tryin' ta help? Are they all wicked?"

"A man with authority and influence is a man who is properly suited and well-spoken, not some beggar who would take the meager belongin's of impoverished travelers. Look at them runnin' off, leavin' pieces of paper with false addresses."

"Oh, Eamon, are there no honest men ta help us?" Maureen began to sob.

"Wife, these be no better than hooligans. Sure an' there are honest men. We jist hafta find them." He smiled and hugged her. "Do not worry, me darlin'. We will be jist foine. Now, Sean, pick up our bundles and let us be goin' into the City. This is America an' thankful 'tis we should be. The Lord has taken us out of purgatory."

He drew his wife close and took his son's hand. They walked slowly along the cobblestone streets, depressed by the hovels and decrepit tenements. Their eyes scanned the filth and squalor. Maureen shook her head. "Oh, Lord, would ya look at this place. We have come from dirt to more dirt!"

Children in rags swarmed around them, begging for coins or anything else. Maureen knelt in front of a little girl who was mimicking the older ones, chanting a "begging rhyme". "Oh, little darlin', God love ya. We have nothin' ta spare. 'Tis sorry I am." The little waif wailed and soon a gang of urchins circled the McCulloughs, shouting obscenities at them and blaming them for the little girl's tears. Within moments, others were milling about, taunting and threatening the now frightened family.

A tall, black youth approached the beleaguered McCulloughs. He yelled at the rowdy group. "Hey, you troublemakers, go on home where y'all belong." The youth was tall for his thirteen years— over six feet—and large and sinewy, with a voice to match. The unruly gang quickly dispersed.

"Thank you kindly." Eamon offered a handshake. "We are the McCulloughs."

The handshake was returned. "I'm called Reese. Did you jest get off the boat?"

Eamon nodded.

"Well," Reese continued, "there's a lot to learn about keepin' alive in this place. Maybe I kin help you folks."

"Would you know where we can find rooms?" Maureen asked. Her display of confidence in this stranger surprised Eamon—and herself.

"Lady, these are mean streets full of mean people. I kin tell you are Irish folks . . . lots of them here. This old lady I work for, she's Irish. Rents rooms . . . might take y'all in, if you can pay her."

The McCulloughs exchanged glances. Eamon spoke up. "We have only a few coin but we were promised a pound each when we land. We jist hafta find the office that has been set up ta do this. By any chance, have you heard of such a place?"

Reese shook his head sadly. "I hear that story every time a shipload of foreigners arrives. There ain't no office, no money waitin' . . . jest strugglin' and fightin' to stay alive."

A cry escaped Maureen's lips. She crossed herself.

Eamon shushed her. "Darlin', 'twill all do soon enough." Turning to Reese, "Would you be kind enough ta take us ta your lady?"

"Sure." Reese picked up the bag Maureen carried. "I'll take this for you."

Eamon and Sean carried theirs and followed Reese through the slum to Mrs. O'Rourke's tenement. In the streets, pigs roamed loose, foraging for food, and even some cattle wandered about. Cardboard shanties dotted the landscape.

Eamon was worried. "Tell me, Reese, why are things so bad? We heard only good things from others who came before."

"Mr. McCullough, there are so many arrivin' every day, most of the time with nothin' more than the clothes on their backs . . . and lots of them sick, too. Most that come only know how to farm, that's all, and there sure ain't no farms around here.

"What can a man do ta care for his family then?" Eamon asked.

"If y'all are willin' to work there's animal slaughterin', horse skinnin', bone boilin' and glue makin'—if y'all can stand the smell!" Reese grimaced.

"Is that what you are afta doin'?" Eamon started to ask about wages, but Reese's answer cut him short.

"I'm pretty lucky, I guess. I work for Mrs. O'Rourke, takin' care of her roomin' house . . . fixin' things, collectin' rents and runnin' her errands. My momma worked for her for a few years 'til she died of the typhus. The missus promised to look after me and that old lady sure did keep her word . . . but she does work me hard." He laughed good-naturedly. After they walked a few more blocks, Reese called out, "Here we are—Mrs. O'Rourke's 'palace'!"

The McCullough's looked at the old brick building. The ravages of time and neglect had taken their toll. The edifice was in shambles. Reese sensed what thoughts must be racing through the minds of his new found friends. "It's not as bad as it looks." He tried to assuage them. "Compared to tents and cardboard shacks . . . well, anyhow, that's why we call this place the 'palace'." He laughed again. "Come on, I'll bring y'all up to meet Mrs. O, that's what everyone calls her."

When they entered the building, they were appalled by the sight of a group of disorderly men loafing about in an area apparently used as a grog shop. Most of them were drunk. Voices were raised in song and obscene jokes were being bandied about. There was a saucer of free tobacco on the end of the counter to which 'clients' were helping themselves.

Maureen was aghast. "Lord save us, what have we here?"

Reese said, "Don't y'all fret none. This is nothin' to worry about . . . jest some men tryin' to forget their troubles. This kind of socializin' goes on all the time."

Maureen put her arm around her son's shoulders and turned him toward her so he would not witness the scene. Her eyes reflected hopelessness as she turned to look at Eamon who, at that moment, was finding the playful drunks amusing. His attitude changed when he saw his wife's scowl.

"Jest follow me up these stairs," Reese quickly suggested, "to Mrs. O's quarters. Y'all will be settled in real soon, I hope."

A loud, cheerful voice yelled, "Come in" when Reese knocked.

Mrs. O sat in a large overstuffed chair, well designed to hold her corpulent body. She did not bother to get up. Reese introduced the bedraggled trio who, by now, were wishing they would be allowed to stay, at least for the night, for they were exhausted.

"Well, now, are ya prepared to pay rent if I grant ya a place?

Eamon was fast to say, "We have a little coin but the lad and I will be gettin' work right away . . ."

Mrs. O'Rourke interrupted. "What makes ya so sure? You are a real Irishman, lookin' on the bright side. It's not so easy, my man."

Maureen said, "Perhaps I could help you with the cleanin' and washin'. We are not lazy, Mam. We are hard workin' farm people . . ." Her voice trailed off.

"I will work, too," Scan added cagerly.

"Oh, Lord love ya, lad." She patted Sean's head. Something about the McCulloughs touched her heart—the delicate though worn features of the woman, the concern on the man's face and the sweetness of the boy's expression. "Ya know, I like your spunk."

Passing through the hallway, where most of the doors were open to capture a fleeting breath of air, the McCulloughs were shocked by the numbers of people crowded into small, dismal rooms. Maureen whispered to Eamon, "'Tis a pigsty, almost as bad as what we have come from."

Finally, at the end of one of the dank hallways, Mrs. O stopped and fiddled with a large ring of keys. "Don't know why I'm bein' so good but I'm lettin' ya have the best." She flung the door open and lit the gas lamp on the side wall next to it. Two beds stood at opposite ends of a 9x12 room. A small, rickety table with two chairs graced the middle, and an ancient washstand with a basin in its center braced itself against an empty wall. A stained, eroded mirror hung above it. Soiled, peeling wallpaper, hanging in musty shreds, decorated the room.

"Outhouses are out back in the yard," Mrs. O announced. "Usually get at least six people in here but I like ya, so ya can have it—and tell ya what," she addressed Maureen, "if ya can be up bright and early every day to help with the chores, ya don't have to pay me rent until the husband here earns some money, ta speak of."

The McCulloughs were torn between despair and necessity. They knew they faced far greater hardships out on the street. Perhaps this was Providence and they should be grateful. Maureen spoke first. "We thank you kindly, Mam, and will not be a burden, fer sure . . ."

Eamon added, "You will not be sorry, I promise."

Sean echoed, "Fer sure, fer sure, Mrs. O."

The old lady beamed at him. Then in a rare display of generosity said, "Come on, darlin's, we'll have a cup of tea and you can tell me all about yourselves. Reese, put the kettle on."

"Thank you, Jesus," Maureen whispered under her breath.

CHAPTER IV

*T*HE *AREA IN which Mrs. O'Rourke's tenement 'flourished' was known as the Five Points, so named because of the points created by the intersection of Park, Worth and Baxter Streets. Within walking distance, Mulberry Street curved around one corner of its perimeter. A long time had passed since the tinkle of cowbells was heard coming over the hill and across green meadows. Today there was only the sound of the bells on the rag pickers' carts. The clustered tenements around the Bend were the worst and of these Mrs. O'Rourke's was the best. Most of the tenantry and many of the landlords were Irish and referred to the district as the "Bloody Sixth" ward. Others referred to the Sixth Ward as Shantytown or Little Ireland. It was bounded by Broadway on the west; Chatham Street on the south; Canal Street on the north; and, on the east, by the Bowery. The area had been primarily German but, as they prospered, the Germans left and many moved to Yorktown on the Upper East Side.*

The McCulloughs settled into a routine of long hours of work, meager rations and little rest. Maureen scrubbed and washed for the landlady. Eamon got a job on the docks as a longshoreman. "'Twill not be fer long, Luv," he would tell his wife, all the while wondering how they could ameliorate their circumstances.

Because she had grown fond of Sean, Mrs. O kept him busy running her errands or accompanying her on visits to the marketplace. "We'll go over ta Fulton Market," she would say, "for some fresh fruit and vegetables and some nice cuts of meat."

Sean looked forward to these visits. The huge marketplace fascinated him. Mrs. O delighted in his spontaneous outcries as he gazed at the array of items. "Oh, my eyes have never looked upon such wonderful things . . . only sorry potatoes most of my life."

"Ya poor darlin'." She hugged him. "There'll be no more of that." She always rewarded him with fruit, vegetables and a generous cut of meat. "Take this to yer folks and tell them Mrs. O says to enjoy it."

One day, Eamon said, "Sean, 'tis proud I am of you, lad. You are working hard to help us but I think we had best look into some edycation fer you. I hear there are public schools in the City. We have got to see to it."

Maureen interrupted. "Oh, no, Eamon. Not the public school! I am afraid he will be exposed to Protestant thinkin'. That is what I heard some of the women sayin' the other day."

He smiled at her. "Do not be worryin' about that. The boy must learn. I will be seein' to it soon.

It wasn't long before Maureen confronted her husband. "I should have known better than ta listen ta you. That book they are usin' in the school—the McGuffey reader—describes the white, Anglo-Saxon Protestant as the model American. My Sean will be a model American and a good Catholic, at that. I will not have him attendin' a school where Catholics are denied the use of their own bible and cannot say their own prayers."

There was a moment of silence in Eamon's corner. He knew better than to argue that point with his wife. "All right, Luv. I will take Sean over ta the Sisters of the Sacred Heart Mission and enroll the boy. Will you be happy with that?"

Maureen folded her arms across her chest, her face radiant with success. "Fer sure," she replied, "darlin', fer sure."

Sometimes, on a Sunday, when the McCulloughs had a little time to themselves, they walked through the neighborhood. "Jist look at the crowds," Maureen would say, "and the nastiness of the streets. Some people are livin' in nothin' more than sheds." She often commented on the odious and degrading sights. "Lord, does the sun ever shine here? Is there a breath of fresh air to be had?"

There was no room for the sun's rays, blotted out by the hanging clotheslines that breached the distances across streets between the tenements, and any wisp of air attempting to circulate in that vast sewer of filth was obliterated by the stench of death and decay.

One Sunday, Eamon suggested, "Let us go fer a walk out of this area. I am tired of lookin' at back alleys and stable lanes."

At first, their curiosity led them through similar neighborhoods but, after an hour or so, they came to lower Fifth Avenue.

Maureen exclaimed, "Oh, Lord!" at the sight of the horse drawn streetcars wending their way uptown.

"Can we follow this avenue and see where it takes us? Can we, Da?"

Laughing at his son's suggestion, Eamon answered, "That is an adventure for anither day. I think we had best find our way back before dark." Seeing the look of disappointment on the boy's face, he put his arm around his shoulder and pointed upward. "Look, boy, we found the sun!"

Even though Five Points was reputed to be the worst slum in New York, most of its residents were hard working people. The McCulloughs soon became acquainted with many of them and their existence fell into a pattern that reflected their united struggle to survive. Maureen and Eamon worked long, hard hours and even Mrs. O's favorite—Sean—spent most of his time tending to his 'mentor's' wishes. Life became a bit more bearable as time passed because there was some money coming in and their expenses were minimal, thanks to Mrs. O's generosity.

One evening, Eamon approached her. "Mrs. O'Rourke, I know how fond you are of Sean and 'tis thankful I am for all you have done ta help us . . ." he hesitated.

"Well, what are ya tryin' ta say? I know you are grateful. You and yours have said so a million times. Come now, out with it— and call me Mrs. O!"

He cleared his throat. "Mrs. O, I want my son ta have a better life as a man than I have had and that can only be accomplished if the lad gets some edycation. Here he has the chance ta do so. It costs some money, but I mean ta register him in a public school—Maureen has finally agreed—with your permission, of course. I do not wish ta offend you . . ."

"Enough! I love the boy, too, as if he were me own. You're thinkin' right for the lad. So, it's off to school with him. I'll miss his company, the little devil." She chuckled. "Anyway, I still have Reese to help."

"Oh, God bless you. We thank the Good Lord everyday fer sending us ta your door. 'Twas a lucky day that Reese found us." He choked up.

"Out with ya now. Send the boy to me. I've somethin' for him."

Attending school was an extraordinary experience for Sean, who had done nothing in his young life in Donegal but plant and harvest. He attended the local school occasionally and only when he could be spared from his chores. The English sponsored schoolhouse was several miles from the farm and he had to walk the distance. Now, in the public school in New York, he did not have far to go. Exposed to other ethnic groups, his world was no longer Irish. Sean applied himself well. His eagerness to acquire knowledge was not lost on his teacher, who was more than happy to spend extra time after classes to answer any of his questions.

Every evening, as the family sat at supper, Sean enthusiastically detailed what had been studied that day. His parents listened, in awe, interjecting "oh's" and "ah's" as the boy spoke.

Maureen commented to Eamon, "Do you see how inspired the lad is? He will be a lawyer or a teacher, fer sure. 'Tis eloquent, he is. Eamon, you did right ta insist on the public school. So far, I have not heard anything ta worry about."

Eamon knew she was alluding to her fear of exposure to Protestant thinking. "Right, my luv. Do not worry. 'Twill do. Now,

I have something ta tell you. Today on the dock while I was unloadin' from this packet that come into port, some fella approaches me and says, 'Could I have a word with you?' About what? I ask."

'Some of the men have been thinking about organizing, you know, joining the union.'

"Sure and I do not know what you are talkin' about," I answered.

"He whispers ta me, 'There's to be a meeting at nine o'clock this Friday night at the old warehouse down by the river at South Street. Why don'tcha come and find out what it's all about. Just don't be telling anyone, okay?'

"Maureen, I heard some talk amongst the other longshoremen about organizin' but I really do not grasp the meanin' of it and no one had approached me, until now. I promised I would try ta be there. Now, Luv, what do I do? I do not want ta get mixed up in anything that will put us in danger. I hear these men are a rough bunch."

After a moment, she answered, "Why not go ta the meetin' and listen ta what they hafta say. If you feel 'tis a good thing, join up. If you find cause fer alarm, tip yer hat and leave. 'Tis a free country."

Eamon laughed. "You sure learn fast, darlin'. You sound like an American already."

That Friday night, at 9 o'clock, Eamon entered the warehouse on the dock at South Street. He hesitated for a moment, cap in hand, as he scanned the huge floor of the building, not knowing how to proceed. Suddenly a booming voice called to him and Eamon faced the stranger who had whispered to him on the dock. "Welcome, friend, I'm Paddy O'Shaughnessy. And you . . ."

"Eamon McCullough." He shifted uneasily from one foot to the other.

Paddy gave him a resounding pat on the back. Well now, I'll introduce you to the boys. We'll be starting the meeting soon. He pointed to several men, rattling off names so quickly, Eamon found it difficult to retain even one. All he could do was to acknowledge each with a nod of his head.

Within a few minutes, a tall stocky man—his ruddy face crowned with a full shock of silver hair—stepped up to the platform at the front of the assembly and took his place behind the lectern. Everyone applauded wildly and then fell silent at a signal from the speaker. Paddy whispered to Eamon, "That's Mike Purcell, he's our leader and organizer." Eamon looked bewildered. Paddy just squeezed his arm and turned toward the speaker with a look of admiration. Mr. Purcell began to speak.

"Brothers, I welcome you to this important gathering. Some of you know me, some of you don't, but we all know why we're here." His voice rose. "Am I right, brothers? Do we know why we are here?" There followed a burst of enthusiasm and shouts of "Brotherhood" rang loud and clear. Purcell signaled for silence. "A decent wage for a decent day's work, that's why we're here and that's what we want! We won't stand for the exploitation of the poor immigrant workers!" There was a stomping of feet and shouts of approval. "Tonight, we are going to hear from a few of the boys working the docks. After you hear their tales of woe, you'll find good enough reasons to join our cause."

Eamon reacted when Purcell mentioned the Canal Street docks. He recognized several of the men who were about to speak. One by one, each told his story of long, hard hours of back-breaking work, for minimal hourly wages, which seemed to get lower as time went on, with more and more newly arrived emigrants put on the job for less wages. As Eamon listened, he was shocked to hear them condone acts of violence against the shipping lines. Why they could all go to jail! What would their families do then?

Mike Purcell's voice interrupted his train of thought. " . . . and I want the pledge of every living one of you here tonight that you will support us in whatever action we find it necessary to take. ARE WE TOGETHER IN SOLIDARITY!" There was a stomping of feet again and shouts of "solidarity" rent the air.

Paddy turned to Eamon, who did not join in the zeal displayed by the others. "Well, laddie, are you with us?"

Stammering, Eamon replied, "I do not know . . . I cannot be sure . . ."

A few men standing nearby overheard the conversation and moved toward them. One of them grabbed Eamon by the shoulder. "What the hell's the matter with ya? Aren't ya sick of the long, hard hours of laborin' like an animal and gettin' wages so low, ya can't provide a decent place for your loved ones?"

Emotions were running high around him. Eamon answered as tactfully as he could. "I will hafta be thinkin' it over. I do not want ta do anythin' ta lose me job . . ."

He was cut short by a blast from another fellow—a large, burly brute with a wicked gleam in his eye. "What are you saying, you fool? The way you're working now, your dear wife and family will be sitting up front with the undertaker at your funeral."

His remarks were cut short by the interference of a neatly dressed, mustachioed young man, who quietly cautioned, "Come now, Billy boy. No use being so unfriendly. You'll give this man the wrong impression of what we're attempting to accomplish." He turned to Eamon, extending his hand. "Eddie Driscoll".

"Eamon McCullough, Mr. Driscoll."

"Pleased to meet you, Mr. McCullough. Why don't we listen to more of what the speakers have to say and then we'll talk again. Meanwhile, grab yourself a beer or a cup of coffee, whichever pleases you. I'll be back to speak with you after the meeting."

Eamon nodded and stood there, thinking. This fellow sounds like he's had an education. He speaks well. I wonder what he is doin' with the likes of longshoremen? Paddy interrupted his thoughts. "Whaddya say, Eamon, what will it be—coffee or a nice refreshing brew?"

"Well, I am not a drinkin' man; coffee will do jist foine."

Paddy laughed and slapped him on the back. "Then coffee it is, my friend. Maybe you'll feel like a beer after you've heard more and made up your mind, eh?"

Eamon smiled weakly. He continued to listen carefully to all the speakers, the majority of whom were dockworkers. Then Mike Purcell introduced the guest speaker. "I have the honor of introducing Mr. Edward Driscoll, attorney-at-law, and the advisor to the Federated Association of Dock Workers in New York City."

A lawyer is it, thought Eamon. No wonder he has a silver tongue. Eddie Driscoll later made his way through the crowd and the applause to seek out Eamon, who was standing near the coffee counter with Paddy. "Well," Driscoll said amiably, "have you made the right choice, Mr. McCullough?"

"Sir, with all due respect, I am afraid the right choice fer me will not be the one you will approve."

Driscoll smiled. "A smart man like yourself . . . I'm sure you'll decide wisely."

Eamon was adamant. "I am afraid, Sir, I cannot put meself in danger of losing work. 'Tis too treacherous fer my loved ones. I could even go ta jail, be regarded as a criminal. No—no, Sir, I cannot neglect me duty as a husband and father."

"But, Mr. McCullough, if there were any problems, we would protect you—that's what the union is for—to protect its members."

By now, a circle of men had formed to listen to the debate. Finally, with parting advice to go home and discuss it with his wife and to come to the next meeting, Eddie Driscoll took his leave.

The belligerent onlookers began mumbling insults at Eamon. The large, burly one who had argued with him earlier, grabbed him by the arm, whirling him about. "Ya thick-headed Mick, ya don't know what's good for ya."

Eamon shrugged loose, staring the man down. He repeated, in a voice ready to do battle, "I know this: I will not put my loved ones in jeopardy!" Suddenly, he was grabbed from behind. Two arms hoisted him off his feet, while a fist landed directly on his face. Then, he was out the door, his buttocks hitting the pavement, hard. He could feel blood trickling down his chin and his right eye swelling. "Oh, Jaysus, Joseph and Mary. What have I gotten meself into?"

As he lay there, bewildered and shocked by the turn of events, he could hear the raised voices of anguished men. Fear gripped him. The same fear he had felt when he stood on the quay at Donegal.

Maureen knew things had not gone well when Eamon came through the door at midnight, one eye blackened and swollen, a cut on the lower corner of his lip, and the collar of his shirt, torn. Oh, Jaysus, what have they done ta you? Oh, Eamon darlin', are you hurtin' too much?" She was hysterical.

"Sh-h-h, Luv, do not wake the boy. I am foine. Just a scratch."

She quickly bathed his face with warm water and placed a cold, damp cloth on his wounded eye. Mrs. O, who heard the commotion, came running in. "What the devil happened?

Eamon hesitated at first to give any explanation but she insisted. When he told her about the stranger and the meeting, she looked him squarely in the eye. "My good man, I will tell ya what to do and ya'd best listen. Join up with those boys or your life will be one of misery. I can tell by looking at ya, ya tried to walk away. These men believe that survival in this city is dependent upon solidarity—that's where the strength lies. Ya would do well to think about it. I bid you goodnight."

Maureen put her arms around Eamon. "Come, darlin', let us go ta bed. We will talk in the mornin'. I have a feelin' we must consider Mrs. O's advice. She knows more about these things than we do."

It seemed appropriate, at the moment, to offer a prayer to St. Jude.

CHAPTER V

S EAN WAS REGISTERED in public school and, from time to time, Maureen would ask, "Are you bein' filled with any of them Protestant ideas?"

"Mam, I am a good Catholic boy," he always retorted. "Nothing will change that."

The old landlady missed Sean's companionship. He spent most of his time in school and doing his homework. Little by little, Mrs. O involved Maureen in her frequent visits to the marketplace. She was amazed at the vast selection of food from all parts of the world. "Oh, would you look at that!" Maureen often exclaimed. Whenever she came near some flowers, she would gently touch one and sigh, "Oh, the beauty of it—I cannot help meself . . ." Her voice would trail off.

Such outbursts brought tears to Mrs. O's eyes. She knew Maureen must have been thinking of the years of starving and struggling. To hide her emotion, she would say, brusquely, "Come on now, dearie, there's no time for thinkin' of the past," and would hustle her along.

On these outings, Maureen became familiar with the streets and took note of the inhabitants and their way of life. In the evening, she would recount her observations to Eamon and Sean. "'Tis strange, fer sure. You would think not one soul worked fer a livin'— not the men, anyhow, sittin' about, half of them in their cups. I do not understand them, lettin' their women go cleanin' houses ta put food on the table and them jist sittin' around makin' jokes and laughin' their bloody heads off. 'Tis a shame!"

"Darlin', you are jist seein' a handful of men. There is that kind everywhere. You have gotta see the men workin' with me on the docks . . ."

"Eamon, I am not faultin' all the men in God's creation. It is jist that I would like ta see things better fer all of us. These drunks are draggin' us down. 'Tis a bad reputation they give Irishmen. Why, walkin' down Chatham and Pearl Streets, all a body can see are saloons . . . and the Bowery! Good Lord! Nothin' but more saloons, cheap lodgin' houses and cheap women." Her cheeks flushed.

"Wifey, you are upsettin' yourself about something we cannot control. There are enough of us who are hard workin', so do not worry, Darlin'—we will make a good place fer the Irish." He hugged her as he winked at Sean. "Look here at your own boy. Did you not say that he will be a lawyer someday? That will be foine fer a son of Eire."

Eamon picked her up and spun her around as he sang; "I will take you home, Kathleen . . ."

*   *   *

A good number of Irish male immigrants turned to liquor as a form of escapism from the despicable conditions of the Sixth Ward. But for all that remained in their shanties or in the dark, unhealthy rooms of the tenements, there were those who had come to the "land of promise" and risen above the signs of "NO DOGS, NO IRISH".

One day, while she was sweeping down the hallway, Maureen overheard bits and pieces of a conversation in which Tammany Hall was mentioned several times. One reference in particular stayed in her mind. The voice had said, "We've got to be right proud. 'Tis full of Irishmen and they look out for their own."

Maureen asked Mrs. O, "Can you tell me what this Tammany Hall is?"

"I've been meanin' ta tell ya about it but I keep fergettin'.

Anyway, 'tis a stronghold for Irish politicians who've made their way up the ladder. Maybe ya've heard about the Democratic Party? Well, the Party and Tammany locked up the vote around here. They see to it that the Irish, and other immigrants as well, are naturalized, makin' them American citizens, by hook or by crook." She laughed. "Then they get them to join the Democratic Party, which is a good thing because that's the party of the workin' class and the poor."

"How can we do that—become citizens and join the Party?" Maureen asked.

"I'll talk ta one of the regulars that stops by every week and has a nip at the bar downstairs. He'll see to it for ya. He works for Big Tim Kelly who runs the show in the Bowery, in this Ward. He's a popular figure because he caters to the voters' needs, helpin' with food, rent, pushcart licenses—he even supplies the flowers for funerals. The organization sure is a drivin' force around here."

When Maureen told Eamon about her conversation with Mrs. O and the prospect of becoming naturalized citizens, he was anxious to know more, so he knocked on the landlady's door that evening. "Mrs. O, can I have a word with you?"

"How are ya, Eamon. I don't see much of ya anymore, workin' such long hours."

"Yes, but 'tis necessary. I want to take good care of me loved ones and, with all due respect, maybe move ta a nicer neighborhood someday. Now, please Missus, me wife says that this place, this Tammany Hall, is it?—That there is a gentleman of your acquaintance who can arrange fer us ta become citizens . . ."

Mrs. O explained everything and said, "Don't ya worry none. I'll have him stop by to see ya some evening."

"Oh, thank you kindly. 'Twas a blessed day that Reese found us and brought us here."

Mrs. O laughed heartily. "I'm not sure how 'blessed' it was but I do agree that it was a lucky one—for both of us. Now, man, it's back to your family with ya. I'll have some news soon."

Eamon mumbled some thanks and withdrew. He told his wife and son about his conversation with Mrs. O, that they were to anticipate a visit from one of Tim Kelly's men.

After a few weeks, that visit finally materialized. The usual introductions took place and, under the keen eye of Mrs. O'Rourke, the interview began and concluded within an hour. The McCulloughs were nervous. Here was a Mr. Murphy from Tammany Hall, come to see us nobodies, Eamon thought, as he held Maureen's hand in his.

The man spoke as he filled out some pages before him. "Now, there's just a few questions I need to ask. There's nothin' to be worryin' about. Accordin' to the Naturalization Law of 1790, if you are a free white person, residing in the United States and under its jurisdiction for at least two years, you are eligible for citizenship."

Eamon quickly answered, "Yes, Sir, that we are."

"Give me your full names and the names of your family members, your ages, and place of birth."

The information provided, Mr. Murphy advised them, "Well, 'tis done. Stop by Tammany Hall in three days, at three in the afternoon, and we'll swear you in."

An outburst of thanks and handshaking followed until he extricated himself and made for the door. "Don't forget. Three days. See you at Tammany at three o'clock. Goodnight."

Mrs. O congratulated them. "Wait a moment. I'll be right back." She returned with a bottle of brandy. "Time to celebrate. You will be honest-ta-goodness Americans in seventy-two hours." They toasted and hugged and kissed. Even Sean was allowed a little nip, which immediately made him giggle and hiccough.

Three days later, at three o'clock sharp, the McCulloughs entered Tammany Hall. Maureen was dressed in her Sunday best. Her new hat, adorned with cherries and flowers, framed her beautiful face. The hat was an Easter gift from Mrs. O. Eamon wore his only white shirt, a tie and the dark suit he had purchased at a local store for $2.95. When they were leaving, Mrs. O had remarked, "Ya look like Americans already!"

They stopped at a desk and the receptionist directed them to a room. "Mr. Kelly will see you in a few minutes," said a serious looking young man, in a tailored suit, with a shirt framed by a high, starched white collar. A pair of metal-framed glasses rested on the bridge of his nose.

"Would that be Mr. Tim Kelly?" an astonished Eamon asked.

Maureen flashed him one of her "hold your tongue" looks. Eamon fell silent at once.

"Yes, sir, Mr. Tim Kelly. Please be seated."

They sat down on one of the plush sofas in the elegantly furnished office.

"Would you look at all of them bookcases around the walls and the beautiful desk and leather chairs." Maureen was wide-eyed. "I bet every piece of wood in here is solid mahogany . . . and them beautiful lamps! Who pays fer all this, I wonder."

The huge door in the far corner of the chamber opened and an enormous man, well over six feet tall, entered. He had the physique of a prizefighter—muscles rippling under his shirtsleeves (he wore no jacket) and a neck thick above his expensive high-collared silk shirt. He gave the impression that he was accustomed to fine cigars and expensive liquor. His graying hair was groomed to perfection, as was his mustache, which turned up at the corners, courtesy of some applied wax. His eyes sparkled with a keen alertness.

"Good day, friends," he boomed at them. "Welcome. You've been highly spoken of, and for." He shook hands with them. "Before we get to the swearin' in, tell me a little about yourselves and the 'auld sod'."

Eamon worried he might say something to spoil things. He spoke honestly about their struggles and upheaval from Donegal, describing the horrendous crossing to America, and of their present situation and his dreams for the future.

All the while, Kelly observed him closely, occasionally casting an eye in the direction of Maureen. "Lord," he said, "how you people have suffered. I admire your pride and your ambition.

Eamon, you're a fine man and if I can ever be of help, just give me a call. Now—let me tell you about the Democratic Party and sign you up. Then, to the swearin' in."

The McCulloughs walked the short distance from City Hall: up Broadway and down Anthony Street, passing Elm and Centre Streets, to their tenement in Five Points. They were too happy to take their usual notice of the sottish males, the squalid females, and the half-starved urchins on the street. They walked on air.

"Can you believe it, darlin'? We are American citizens! Just watch. Things will go better fer us. And Sean, now you can tell off them rascals at school who have been callin' you 'greenhorn'."

Maureen squeezed her husband's hand. "You are a foine man and have done well fer us."

"Without you, me darlin', I could not have done anythin'." He kissed her right there in the middle of the street. Passersby stared.

She pushed him away, saying playfully, "Well now, sir, would you have everyone thinkin' I am one of them loose women from the Bowery?"

He kissed her again.

CHAPTER VI

S EVERAL MONTHS PASSED without incident. Eamon worried about being approached by the union organizers again, but his concerns were dispelled when an attempt to organize a strike was foiled. The ship owners issued an order that if the workers persisted, the National Guard would be called in. Even though strikes to improve labor conditions had been declared legal, and although national unions of the same craft were growing their memberships, many dock workers (primarily immigrants) were loath to jeopardize their jobs in actions against their employers. There were no further attempts to organize for a while.

"You know," Eamon told Maureen, "'tis glad I am that the trouble has been settled fer now. I can understand how the union is tryin' ta make things better fer us, but I do not have the stomach fer it at this toime—ta be out of work, no. And now that we are citizens, I do not want ta oppose the government."

"I know how you feel, Eamon, but sometimes a man has ta stand up fer what he believes in, or there will niver be change fer the better. Look at the terrible sufferin' all of us went through fer so long, keepin' out silence in Donegal. But I am happy now there has not been trouble."

"Well, there has been plenty of trouble in some places. One of the men, Timmy Mahoney, got a letter from his cousin who is workin' on the Troy and Boston Railroad, up in northeast New York. He writes that the men were promised good terms—some of them spent their last penny to get there—and when they had enough men ta do the work, they kept reducin' the wages until the poor lads were gettin' somethin' like fifty-five cents a day. When they tried ta strike, the authorities called in the National Guard—'tis sad . . . shootin' and all . . . woundin' hard workin' men who want nothin' more than ta feed their families.

"And those that stayed in their shanties . . . ." He shook his head. "Miles and miles of them . . . nothin' but sufferin', especially fer the Irish—treated like slaves, cheated of their pay with overpriced goods, almost worthless coin . . ."

"Eamon," Maureen interrupted, "have you thought about askin' Mr. Kelly about finding you a job? You are killin' yourself. All them long hours and back breakin' work. Mrs. O says many of her customers at the bar work fer Tammany Hall. Maybe . . ."

"Darlin', I know you hate me job as much as I do, but I am bashful ta be askin' Mr. Kelly fer a favor."

"But, Luv, that is exactly what he told you ta do, if ya wanted to."

Eamon knew that when Maureen made a suggestion, it was almost an order, so he promised, "Wifey dear, I will be doin' that as soon as I can spare toime away from the docks. Meanwhile, be patient. I will make you proud yet."

They hadn't spent a Sunday away from Five Points since the walk they took to Fifth Avenue where they watched the horse-drawn trolley. When Eamon told them, "We will be goin' fer a walk to Greenwich Village, after church on Sunday," they were overjoyed. "I have the day off. Only this toime, we are goin' ta Washington Square Park. I hear 'tis a lovely place ta enjoy the fresh air and the trees . . . maybe we will find somewhere ta have a bite ta eat."

Sean was excited. "You know, Da, we learned in school that the arch in the park is a copy of the arch in Paris. It's 77' high and was built to celebrate the hundredth year since our first President was inaugurated."

Laughing and slapping her thighs, Maureen said, "Would you listen ta the Yankee now. What was it you said about the president's in—org—a—I cannot even repeat it!"

"Inaugurated, Mam. It means when he was sworn into office."

"God luv you, Sean. You are as smart as a whip. You are talking like an American already." She kissed him and patted him on the backside.

Embarrassed, he pulled away. "Mam, I'm too old for this little boy stuff."

"Too old, is it? Stuff, is it? Look here, you are me little boy fer always and if I fancy pattin' yer fanny, or kissin' you—well, that is jist what I will do!" She grabbed at his buttocks again.

Sunday was a pleasant day. Comfortable temperatures and a mild breeze dissipated some of the odors that usually pervaded the neighborhood. All morning Sean raced around. After washing, he dressed in his "good" Sunday suit, the one Mrs. O had so kindly purchased for him. He yelled to his parents, "We'd better hurry so we make early Mass, then we'll have the rest of the day for our walk."

"Son, do not be rushin' so; we have plenty of toime. ''Tis only eight o'clock in the mornin' and we are attendin' the ten o'clock Mass, leavin' lots of toime fer our adventure."

From behind a dressing room screen, Maureen called out. "I will be ready in a minute. Sean, keep yer pants on!"

Father and son looked at each other. Eamon had to laugh at the look that crossed Sean's face. "Yer Mam is gettin' more Americanized by the day."

When she stepped out from behind the screen, both Eamon and Sean could not help but gasp. "Darlin', you are a thing of beauty ta behold," Eamon declared.

Maureen blushed. "We have Mrs. O ta thank fer the new wardrobe. She is surely kind." She picked up her new straw hat, trimmed with ribbons and flowers, and pinned it into place on her beautiful blonde hair. "We have come a long way from the 'hunger', thank the Lord."

After Mass at the little neighborhood Catholic church, the

McCulloughs began their odyssey: from Bayard, Park and Baxter Streets, past all the dilapidated shops, stands, and ash barrels serving as counter tops where vendors sold everything from tobacco to strange looking fish. Sausage hung from doorways. Women, with bundles of firewood on their heads and vegetables in their aprons, carried babied in slings, which hung from their necks. The McCulloughs made their way to Mulberry Street (which looked more like a marketplace in southern Italy than a New York street). They took pleasure in seeing people enjoying the camaraderie and good weather.

"When the sun shines, it gives people a chance ta escape their ugly, crowded living conditions. Them Eyetalians are surely a happy-go-lucky lot. Look at them laughin' and kissin' and chatterin' away. I heard a funny story from one of the boys at the dock. There was this dead goat lyin' on the road on Pell Street and the police at the Elizabeth Street station were told about it. By the toime they brought the offal-cart ta pick up the unfortunate animal, it had disappeared. Turns out an Eyetalian had taken it ta be used at a back-alley feast of sorts."

They all had a good laugh. Then Sean asked, "Da, could we have a bite to eat? I'm gettin' hungry."

"We will, Son, when we get over ta the Village. 'Tis nicer there. I have saved some coin fer us ta have a lunch somewhere. Be patient."

They cut across to Broadway and up to Washington Square. The cobblestone streets were lined with trees and two-story brick houses. Horse-drawn carriages dotted the landscape; street lamps, which were lighted by gas at night, stood like silent sentinels.

"Oh, Eamon, 'tis a different world up here. Everything is so clean and orderly . . . and how foine are the men and women!" She smoothed down the front of her dress, self-consciously, and adjusted her hatpins.

He was quick to say, "And you are lookin' foine, Luv. I know you are thinkin' otherwise but there is no need ta. We McCulloughs are jist grand altogether!" Maureen and Sean always enjoyed his optimism. "Now," he continued, let us find a place a eat and then we will sit on a bench in the park and watch the upper crust."

On the way home, Eamon said, "You know, I am thinkin' 'tis toime we opened a back account. The Emigrant Industrial Bank is well-spoken of fer protectin' the funds of Irish laborers and fer sendin' relief ta the old country."

"But, Eamon, we only have about twenty-five dollars put away. Will the bank take that?"

"They will take that and less, and they are payin' interest on the money, too."

In answer to his mother's puzzled look, Sean explained "interest".

"We will do it at once." Then changing the subject, Maureen asked, "Eamon, do you think we can ever live in a lovely place such as some we saw today?"

"Darlin', that is jist what I am thinkin'. Ya know, I believe 'tis toime ta ask Mr. Kelly fer a favor."

"Oh, Eamon, will you? I am so happy you decided ta go ta him." This time, she was the one to do the hugging and kissing right there in the middle of Broadway.

"Sure and you are a loose woman!" Eamon laughed as he returned her kiss.

Not too long after Eamon's promise to see Big Tim Kelly, Maureen decided to approach Mrs. O. "I do not want ta trouble you but could I ask a favor?"

"Child, what is the matter? These last few weeks, I've been noticin', ya always seem on the verge of sayin' somethin' but don't."

"I would not be askin' but you know how hard Eamon works down on the docks . . . the poor man is wearin' himself out . . . and now he says lately the big ships have been landin' over on the west side at the Hudson River. A lot of men have lost their jobs here and Eamon fears he could be let go at any toime." Maureen was wringing her hands. "Anyway, I was wonderin', do you think Mr. Murphy could arrange fer Eamon ta see Mr. Kelly about a job?"

"I know yer man pretty good. With all the trouble and sufferin' ya been through, he conducts himself like a gentleman—and don't complain none, either. He should have a chance at somethin' better . . . somethin' that'll elevate the man . . . make him feel he's got a chance ta do good by his loved ones."

Maureen grasped her hand. "Mrs. O, you are so kind."

"Hush now, I've been thinkin' about it. Your little boy is growin' up into a find lad and his father should be able to improve your circumstances."

Misty-eyed, Maureen nodded and dabbed at the tears brimming over.

Mrs. O continued, "Let's see what Big Tim can do fer Eamon. We've got ta prepare fer your future. I think the McCulloughs have paid their dues ta Five Points."

"I do not understand . . ." Maureen looked questioningly at the old lady.

"Ya'll see, child, ya'll see. I'm not so old that I can't make some plans. But, I'm not tellin' ya anything yet. We'll go one step at a time. Now, let's get downstairs ta the bar and tidy things up a bit before the evening trade comes by."

Maureen's mind raced, trying to capture the significance of the landlady's remarks, but she just became more confused. She felt an excitement within her that she had never experienced before. It took several minutes before she recognized the emotion. Impulsively she reached out her arms to envelop Mrs. O and kissed her on the cheek.

"Oh, go on with ya now, foolish girl. Nothin's happened yet. Ya act like someone gave ya a prize."

"That you did, Missus, that you did: hope, you have given me hope.

This time it was the old lady who wiped away tears.

Eamon stood, cap in hand, in Tammany Hall, as the same receptionist welcomed him and the same secretary advised, "Please sit down, Sir. Mr. Kelly will be with you momentarily."

How foine he speaks, thought Eamon. Such proper English and so polite. My Sean is learnin' quickly. It will not be long before he will dress like this fella and speak like him, too. Sean will make a good livin'—not like his greenhorn father!

Eamon, suddenly overcome by a feeling of inadequacy, almost bolted when he heard a loud, familiar voice. "Well, well now, Mr. McCullough, how are you? Good to see you again."

"I am pretty good, Sir. But, I have big concerns regardin' me family sityation."

"Why's that . . . uh, Eamon is it?"

"Yes sir. You see, work on the East River docks is becomin' more and more scarce fer a lot of us men. The shippin' business has shifted ta the docks up on the Hudson."

"Are you still workin'?"

"Yes sir. Same long hours and small money. and now, with the fear of bein' laid off . . ."

"Eamon, you impressed me when you came here with your lovely wife a year or so ago to become citizens. I could tell you were a hard-workin', God-fearin' man. That's why I told you to call me if you needed help. You're a proud man, I know, but I'm glad you decided to ask. Here in our precinct, we look after our own . . . kinda like a security blanket for the Irish . . . like the parish is."

Eamon nodded. "Yes, I have seen the help you have given to some of the families."

"How's that fine lad of yours and the wife. Well, I hope."

"Oh, very well, Mr. Kelly. Scan is goin' ta the high school this year and Maureen is foine."

"Is she still workin' for old Mrs. O'Rourke? She is too lovely a lady to do such work."

Eamon's face reddened. "I am hopin' ta put an end ta that, if I can get some work that pays a decent wage." He was surprised at his own bluntness but he did promise Maureen that he would be persistent.

Big Tim sensed Eamon's embarrassment and anxiety. "What would you think of a job like Mr. Murphy's—representin' the organization in the neighborhood. We'll assign you to a couple of streets. You will be the eyes and ears of the Party, sort of overlookin' things and reporting back to this office."

Eamon couldn't believe his ears.

"And," Big Tim continued, "you'll be on the payroll at $25 a week. Whaddya say?"

Eamon was overwhelmed, too shocked to answer. He had to work at hard labor for long hours to make that kind of money. Finally, finding his voice, he expressed his thanks. "You will not be sorry. I am ever so grateful. Jist tell me what it is I am ta do and I will do me best."

They spent the next few hours together. Big Tim introduced him to some of the other "ward heelers" and party members employed by Tammany. Then he personally escorted Eamon to the streets he wished him to keep an eye on and contact with the residents, who would report any goings on that were of interest or importance to Tammany.

"It's like a society within a society where the party and the parish provide a feelin' of economic stability—and even hope for improvement."

Eamon said, "I will do me best. A man could not ask fer a better way ta earn a livin': honest work and helpin' his own."

Big Tim smiled broadly and shook Eamon's hand. "Good man!"

CHAPTER VII

E AMON HAD BEEN on the job for a few months when, one evening, he sat at the table in a pensive mood as he stirred his cup of tea and added sugar. His eyes followed the little whirling tealeaves as they escaped from the strainer.

"You are in deep thought tonight, husband. Are you troublin' over somethin'?"

Shifting uneasily in his chair, Eamon hesitated, then said, "I do not understand some of the goin's on about the Negroes. There are none in the Party because they not have the vote, and the boys at Tammany are not opposin' their return to the South. They are slaves, they say."

Maureen broke in, "Look around you. Are any of us more than that?" She lowered her voice. "With all due respect to Mrs. O."

"Anyway," Eamon continued, "the Party looks at them as competition fer jobs and opposes any more of them comin' North."

"I guess," Maureen answered, "'tis a good thing Reese is workin' fer Mrs. O. She protects the boy. Do you think his mama was one of them runaway slaves?"

"Who knows? I have niver asked about her, have you? Yer always gabbin' with the missus—maybe she will say somethin' about it. Anyway, I am not fancyin' the idea of them anti-abolitionists traipsin' around here. I heard they kidnapped a couple of escaped slaves—two men and a woman—and jist last week returned them to their owners. Why, that is worse than anythin' we have known. Back in the old country, the landlords owned our land, but they did not own us."

Maureen interjected, her voice animated. "Did they not! Burned our homes ta the ground and sent us ta the hell of the coffin ships and us not bein' able ta resist any of it!" She raised her handkerchief to her nose.

"Come now, Luv, I hate it when you are with the long face and so agitated." He pounced upon the opportunity to change the subject. "Darlin', there will be a picnic next Sunday at the part near Tammany and we are invited ta go."

"A picnic! How charmin' is that? But wait, do we hafta contribute any money to it? You know we are savin' every cent fer Sean's edycation."

"No, no. 'Tis a treat fer all of us who work fer the Party and their families. Mr. Kelly says 'tis one of our benefits. So what say you, Luv?"

She reacted with a typically feminine question: "What will I wear, Eamon?"

"Yer Sunday best, of course, me darlin'."

They both had a good laugh at that because their "Sunday best" was the only "best" they had.

Now that Eamon was making a better living, he did not want Maureen working in the tenement anymore. "We will manage jist foine and we will pay Mrs. O rent from now on."

At first, Maureen balked at the idea. She discussed the matter with the landlady who agreed with Eamon. "Ya've worked hard enough, girl. 'Tis time ya did some improvin' of yourself. When Sean has some time ta spare, 'twould be good for ya ta sit down and learn a bit more readin' and writin' . . . and I'll not be takin' rent from ya. Yer like family ta me—and I've got me plans."

These secret plans of Mrs. O's puzzled Maureen but she never dared ask outright what they were. All Mrs. O would do is smile mysteriously and change the subject. "Maureen, I am happy ya live here and I can depend upon ya, when I need it."

*   *   *

One day, two strangers stood in front of Mrs. O's tenement, staring at the Rooms to Let sign that hung from a metal hook on the front of the building. They observed the elderly woman standing outside with a tall, muscular black youth and heard her ask, Reese, would ya be a good lad and get me shoppin' basket? I must have left it on the counter in the bar."

"Sure thing, Mrs. O." The boy vanished momentarily and then reappeared, basket in hand.

"Your dear mother would have been proud of the fine man ya growin' up ta be. Now let's be about our business." They soon disappeared into the crowds along the street.

The strangers could not believe their uncanny luck. "I do believe he's that boy on our list," one of them said.

His companion nodded. "Well, let's rent ourselves a room. Seems like a mighty nice place."

"I do believe that would be wise."

They smiled and entered the building. A sign on the door their right read "Office". A courteous Maureen greeted them. "Might I be of help?"

"Well, pretty lady, might we see what sleepin' quarters y'all have to offer?"

She blushed and said, "Follow me, if you please." To herself, she thought, strange-lookin' men. The clothes they wore—the leather boots and large hats—she did not find them familiar—and the way they spoke with that slow drawl. She showed them the available quarters. "The rent will be five dollars a week fer each of you. That would include coal fer the fireplace."

"Well, that's jest fine, little colleen. We'll take it." Money exchanged hands. At the moment, all Maureen could think of was how happy she was to have been of help to Mrs. O while she was gone for the day.

Later that evening, when they were all having supper together, Maureen recounted her success in renting the room. When she described the new tenants, Mrs. O became apprehensive. "Ya say they looked and sounded different from anyone around here? Why do I have the feelin' they spell trouble . . . like what ya said Eamon was talkin' about the other night . . . about them anti-abolitionists comin' up here, stirrin' up hard feelin's. Maybe that's who they are."

"Oh, missus, I hope I did not do wrong. The last thing I want ta do is make problems."

"Don'tcha worry yer little head. I can handle things." She turned to Reese. "Finish yer dinner and go ta yer room. Stay out of sight 'til I get the lowdown on these men."

As she hurried out, after her tea, Sean was just returning from the library. "Hello, dear boy," she called and charged down the hallway. She hastened to the newly rented room and knocked vigorously. There was no answer. Where were the blitherin' idiots, she wondered. She promised herself she would check on them first thing in the morning.

*   *   *

When Reese entered his room, he was not aware of the two men standing in the shadows until he heard the harsh whisper, "Don't open your mouth, boy, or y'all are one dead nigger."

Too stunned to speak and frightened, Reese obeyed. He noticed that they had messed up his room. They tied his hands behind his back and quickly ushered him out of the room, through the back door of the cellar and into the alleyway where a truck with its motor running, waited.

"Y'all are goin' home, boy," one of them said, sarcastically. "Too bad your mammy ain't here no more. She'd enjoy the ride home."

Reese flinched. He understood immediately. Sarie had told him stories of the plantation and why they had to run away. She had spoken of the "Underground Railroad" and the help they received from both black and white folks as they escaped North. These years with Mrs. O, they had enjoyed a sense of security. He continued to feel that same security in spite of his mother's death five years ago. Now, he wondered, how could this happen? Who were these men? Before he was blindfolded, he caught a glimpse of them—rough, mean-looking. Oh, God, I'm scared, he admitted to himself. He felt like crying but did not.

The motor whined as the driver shifted gears. Soon they were moving. Reese could tell when they were still in the city by the number of turns the truck made and from the familiar sounds and smells. After awhile, it grew quiet, the only sound being that of tires on rough stretches of graveled roads and then, more smoothly, on asphalt highways.

It was difficult to remain stoic. Finally, tears of frustration rolled down his face. Bound and helpless, what chance did he have? As he dealt with his thoughts, he overheard some mumbled words. Good idea . . . Five Points . . . lucky choice. A low chuckle was followed by a loud, sneering voice. "Hey, boy, we all are headin' south, jest where y'all belong." A raucous laugh punctuated Reese's misery. He shuddered.

*   *   *

The first thing, early the next morning, Mrs. O went to check on Reese. She approached his basement room, softly calling his name. She was fond of Reese. He was like a son, her right hand, taking care of the privies in the rear yard, handling the coal for the fireplaces, seeing to it that garbage was properly boxed and set out in front of the building . . . and, of course, he was a companion, as well. Her promise to Reese's mother was something she would never forget.

She remembered how she had taken them in when she found the woman hiding with her young boy in the coal cellar. "Pleeze, pleeze, don' call de police," the woman had begged. "We'll hafta go back to de plantation and de massa will punish us. Pleeze, ah wants mah boy to be free . . ." She had convulsed into tears. "Ah'll do whatever y'all wants. Ah don' keer fo' mahself, its mah son . . ."

Mrs. O had tried to calm her. "Stop yer cryin' now. I'll not cause ya harm. What is yer name and where do ya come from?'

Sobbing subsided into sniffles and whimpers. "Ah'm called Sarie. Ah don' know no other name. Mah boy here is Reese. De massa, Mr. McKnight, was talkin' 'bout sellin' him soon's he growed a little taller. Ah couldn't think 'bout that happenin' . . . bein' widout mah chile. Oh, Lord, no!"

"The dirty bastard!" Mrs. O spat out the words. "There's lot of low things in this world but nothing' lower than someone who would take a child away from its mother. You come with me, Sarie, and tell me the whole story." She had ushered the helpless pair up the stairs to her quarters. Sarie and son soon became part of the fixtures in Mrs. O's palace.

Now, as she tapped on the door, calling "Reese" again, the silence was foreboding. The door opened easily to her touch. She faced a room in disarray. "Oh, Lord, where's the boy? Where've they taken him?" She rushed upstairs to the new tenants' room and pushed the door open. Barely a scrap of anything lay about except for the crumpled, torn page of an old newspaper that lay in the corner. She hastily smoothed out the fragment from the Baltimore Sun and recognized several advertisements for runaway slaves. One stopped her in her tracks. The names "Sari" and "Reese", lined in red ink, jumped up at her. Her mouth gaped as she read, "Ran away on the 17th May, 1854, Sari Gordon, a 28-year old yellow-skinned female, with her 9 year old boy, Reese, from Hampton Farm in Towson, Maryland. A liberal reward is offered."

"Oh, Jesus!" Mrs. O hurried up the stairs, calling, "Maureen, girl, come quick!" She told her, in gasps, that what she feared had happened and showed her the newspaper clipping. "So, there's no doubt 'twas them dirty slave hunters come ta take my Reese. I'll kill the bastard who give him up." Tears coursed down her face.

Maureen tried to comfort her with a promise to have Eamon look into the matter, that he would ask Mr. Kelly for help. "Do not worry. At least, we know the name of the owner and his place. We will get Reese back, fer sure."

Mrs. O held a large handkerchief into which she blew her nose, hard.

When Sean heard them discussing Reese's disappearance, his grief was uncontrollable. He loved Reese. They had developed a close friendship and Sean enjoyed the hours they spent together devoted to teaching Reese how to read and write.

Sean turned to his father. "Da, in class we discussed the problem of the blacks in the South and how they are escapin' to the North. Our teacher spoke of the Underground Railroad and the help they are givin' the runaway slaves. Is there somethin' we can do?"

"Do not worry, Son. I will ask around and we will find Reese."

"I hope so," Maureen said. Mrs. O is beside herself with the grief, the poor dear. We have got ta help."

*　　*　　*

As the truck sped down the road and out of the city limits, the men engaged in a dialogue that aggravated Reese's already depleted spirit. He overheard one say, "Well, we'll be goin' through New Jersey soon. Sure could use a drink and a visit to a toilet. Y'all stop as soon as we get to one of them roadside stops, ya hear?"

The driver agreed. "Sounds like a fine idea. We'll take the blindfold off'n the nigger and let him pee in the woods. Cain't bring him back stinkin' too much. We gotta earn the reward." He snickered.

His companion asked, "Do y'all think it's wise to let him see us and the roads we are takin'?"

"No problem with that, I believe. Niggers cain't read nor write . . . cain't see how's he'd know anythin' . . . cain't read no signs or nothin'."

Within a short time, Reese felt the truck slow down to a halt. He had dozed, fitfully, but now all his senses were alerted. "Come on, boy, y'alls goin' to enjoy a little walk in the woods to relieve yourself." His blindfold was removed. Reese squinted as his eyes adjusted to his surroundings.

The gaslights in front of the little store illuminated a sign: Food and Beverages

"Could I have a drink of water, please?" Reese asked. His tongue and mouth were parched.

"Don't know as they serve niggers here," one of them sneered.

The other advised. "Better git him a drink. Don't want him passin' out on us." He reached for his rifle. An intense fear gripped Reese. They signaled him to walk ahead of them to some nearby trees and underbrush. "Y'all stand where we can see you. Boy, don't make me use this rifle. Y'all behave and a nice, big glass of water will be your reward."

As Reese stood in the thicket, the men did not take their eyes from him as they made obscene remarks and laughed. When they brought him back to the truck, they brought him a cup of water and then bound him up again. It was too dark to make out much of their whereabouts. Reese thought, maybe if they don't blindfold me again, I'll be able to read some signs during daylight . . . see some things that will help me find my way back . . . if I ever have the chance. How lucky it was that Sean had taught him to read and write! So far, all I know is there's a place called Towson, near a city called Baltimore, a place his mother had mentioned. He leaned against the side of the truck and closed his eyes. I'd best get some sleep and be awake at daybreak, he decided.

*   *   *

Gloom had settled over Mrs. O's palace. Everyone was upset by the tragic turn of events. Even the customers at the bar debated how sad it was that the boy was taken. Sure an' somethin's ta be done about this slavery business, was the concensus of opinion.

Eamon discussed it with Big Tim who promised that he would contact 'certain people' who might be in a position to help. He promised nothing else but Eamon had confidence in his employer. On many occasions, he had seen the impossible become a reality.

"You know, my friend," Big Tim said, "I'm not in favor of bringing blacks up here because they are takin' jobs away from the rest of us. But, this bein' a different situation—him bein' like family to Mrs. O and you—I'll do my best."

When Eamon told Mr. O and Maureen, they were overjoyed. "Big Tim will take care of it all. He has connections and knows his way around. You will see, my dears," the old lady said with assurance.

The days passed with a semblance of normality as the McCulloughs and their landlady kept up a relentless pursuit to find a way to get Reese back. One of the merchants with whom Mrs. O did business, traveled up from Washington, D.C. every few months to make deliveries. She persuaded him to go to Hampton Farm on the pretext of buying a "young, strong nigger" to work on his plantation in Washington. "Perhaps ya will see my Reese. I know he's there. Pay any amount they want, but bring him home. I'll pay ya back and then some. Ya have my hand on it."

Mr. McIvey was a man of his word and, after many years of doing business with Mrs. O, he knew "her hand on it" was as solid as a written agreement. "I'll be happy to do my best," he assured her as he shook her hand.

Maureen and Eamon were glad some plan was in place, finally, that might work. Eamon's appeal to Big Tim had brought no results and when be broached the subject, answers were vague. Then one day Big Tim told him, "Now, listen to me, lad. The idea of rescuin' a runaway slave is not sittin' well with the boys. There's a lot of hard feelin' about the Negroes. I don't think it's wise for me, politically, to get involved. Do you understand? I'm sympathetic and all that, but I've got to stand with the Party."

Eamon nodded and hid his terrible disappointment. "Thank you, anyway."

Now Mrs. O's news gave them some hope. Sean listened silently and thought, how bad is that, that Mr. McIvey would have to "buy" Reese in order to bring him home.

CHAPTER VIII

REESE BOLTED OUT of a deep but fitful sleep. The wagon had come to an abrupt halt and he lunged forward, in spite of his restraints. He heard the one called Tom say, "We all will be passin' over into Delaware soon, Fred. Prob'ly make it to Towson, Maryland, by t'morra late afternoon. Sure hope that McKnight fella has the reward handy."

It was broad daylight and Reese paid close attention to the signposts. Would he ever remember them? As they journeyed on, stopping occasionally to water the horses, the two men ate. They gave Reese some bread and water. He wondered about how his mama ever traveled so far with him and who had helped her.

The wagon pulled into Hampton Farm shortly before dusk the next day. A lanky white youth of 20 years approached. "Might I be of some help to y'all?" He appraised the two men and the bound, black boy from a slight distance. "I'm Roland McKnight. My father owns this plantation."

Tom, the larger, huskier one answered, "A pleasure to meet y'all. We done brung back this young nigger who run away from here with his mammy a few years ago."

"And who might that be?" Roland asked.

"His name is Reese and we do believe his mammy was called Sarie."

With a look of disbelief, Roland stepped up closer to the rear of the wagon. "Reese? Is it really—Reese Gordon? I do declare, I never thought I'd lay eyes on y'all again." He shook Reese's hand vigorously.

"It's me, Mr. Roland. Sure didn't recognize you at first, but now I remember . . ." Unable to continue, he sat there recalling how he had trudged alongside his mama as she tended to a white boy, a little older than himself—how they sometimes played games together—how Sarie did the cooking up at the main house and fed them. How jealous he would feel, at times, of the special attention Sarie showered on Roland, even though she explained time and time again that it was her responsibility to take "proper care of the boy 'cause de marsuh own us an' we gotta do what he want, so's we can stay together." Reese never understood the full significance of those words until that awful day when she came into their quarters and frantically tossed items of clothing into a bag. "Son, we gotta leave dis place right now. De marsuh been talkin' 'bout sellin' you soon."

Reese had cried, "Mama, mama, I don' wanna go somewhere widout you, where I don' know nobody . . ."

She had quieted him with the promise, "Ain' nobody takin' my baby from me. We goin' somewhere where we be free." She had hugged and kissed him. "Now, git yo' most precious and fav'rit things to bring wid us." He promptly reached under his bed to retrieve the little wooden dog that Sarie told him his daddy had crudely carved from the branch of an old tree, which stood near their hut. Reese sighed deeply. He had never known his daddy. All he knew was that he was white, worked on the plantation and killed in a road accident.

Roland's voice broke his reverie. "Y'all untie him while I go up to the house for the money."

When he returned, Reese was exchanged for the reward. The two men thanked Roland with a "Glad to be of service to y'all" and drove away. Down the road, Tom took off his hat, scratched the top of his head and exclaimed, "I'll be damned! That McKnight fella looked happy like he was welcomin' a long lost relative."

The elder McKnight was not sentimental about Reese's return but he was enthusiastic about the potential. A good, strong nigger would bring a good price. He instructed his son to assign Reese to one of the log huts, which housed the plantations slaves. The quarters were far from comfortable, most bedsteads consisting of a large board, blanket, and whatever could be scrounged up to serve as a pillow. Roland brought a few extra covers for Reese and expressed how sorry he was about his quarters. "I'll try to get Daddy to give y'all work up at the main house, so's y'all can sleep there. I'm sure glad to see y'all again, my friend."

Reese tried hard to adapt himself. He missed Mrs. O and the McCulloughs and his life in New York. Many nights, he cried himself to sleep but never made his misery obvious. The weekly rations of corn meal, herrings, and pork barely kept him going. As often as possible, Roland would find excuses for bringing Reese up to the house where he would feed him and give him some "extras" to take back to the hut.

After Reese had been there a little over two months, he was approached by Roland one afternoon while he was working in the fields. "Listen, Reese, I can't talk too long 'cause I don't want to arouse any suspicion. Y'all just keep doin' your chores but pay close attention. I'll be leavin' some decent clothes under your bed and there'll be some money in the shirt pocket . . ."

"I don't understand . . ." Reese interrupted.

Roland stopped him, continuing, "Sunday, when everybody is in church, I'll come fetch y'all and drive to the shore. I want y'all to run, Reese, to get away and back to freedom. Y'all will have a good chance to go pretty far in daylight. There's a man— James Carson—who has a cabin in the woods near the river. He'll be on the lookout and waitin' for y'all. Do what he says. Understand?"

Reese nodded. "Why are you doin' this? I don't want you to get in trouble on my account."

"Reese, I heard my daddy say he's 'bout to sell y'all to his friend in Virginia. I can't let that happen. Your mammy was my nanny and we all were like family."

The same fear that enveloped Reese when he was taken from Mrs. O's cellar now gripped him again.

Roland continued, "Come Sunday morning, y'all say to the overseer. 'I'm sick to my stomach. I don' throw'd up this mornin' so many times'. He'll probably say to get into bed and that he'll be by to check on y'all after church. Now, Reese, stay in the hut until y'all hear my low whistle. I'll be outside with my horse and wagon. That'll be your signal to come a runnin' and jump into the cart. Make sure to bring the clothes I leave under the bed."

"Yes sir." Reese's heart pounded. "But suppose the patrols are out watchin'?"

"Don't worry none 'bout them. Even white trash goes to the House of the Lord on Sundays. That is one day they can't steal or collect rewards!" He laughed.

That Sunday, Reese did as he was instructed and soon they were traveling through the woods. Roland gave him some additional advice. "Stay inland as much as possible for the first few hours. Then change your clothes and discard your old ones in the river, first chance y'all get. By the time it grows dark, I calculate, y'all should be near Mr. Carson's cabin. Look for a tall, whiskered man— usually wears suspenders over a brightly colored plaid shirt—carries a rifle and hides a knife in each boot. Wait in the undergrowth. He'll be out there—him and his retriever. The dog'll find y'all but don't be scared; he won't do no harm; he'll just 'retrieve' y'all."

Reese couldn't help but smile in spite of the pulsation in his temples and the uneasiness he felt. "I thank you kindly, Roland. Hope you don't suffer none because of helpin' me."

"God bless, Reese." Roland turned the wagon, slapping the horse gently with the reins.

After several hours of making his way through the woods but always in sight of the shoreline, Reese changed his clothes and disposed of the old ones at a point in the river where the current seemed strong and would carry them away. As dusk fell, he approached a clearing. Cautiously, he crept toward it in the underbrush. At first, he did not see the man, but, all of a sudden, he heard whining and then a loud bark. Before he could move, a large golden retriever had him by the sleeve. A loud voice boomed, "Who are you?"

"Reese, Sir. My name is Reese."

"Come on out here, boy. The dawg won't hurt you. I've been waitin' on you."

Reese slowly followed the dog's lead and within second stood before the imposing figure of James Carson. "Hurry!" he said, "Into the house! The night patrol will be comin' through soon. You'll be safe here for a while. Did you toss your clothes in the river?" Reese nodded. "Good," the man said. "Now get in house."

After sharing a meal, he told Reese to go to the bedroom and get a good night's sleep. "You will be needin' all the strength you can muster for the trip ahead. But, I'll explain in the mornin'. Goodnight, Reese. God be at your side."

Later that night, baying hounds and loud barking echoed across the woods. Mr. Carson came to the bedroom. "Pay no attention to that. They are out lookin' for runaways every night. Prob'ly followed your scent until they got to the river. Them poor hounds must be spinnin' in circles 'cause they can't find the scent no more." He laughed. "Get some sleep. See you in the mornin'."

The next day, Mr. Carson instructed Reese as to what he must do. "I'm handin' 'free papers' to you. Show them to anyone who asks. Can you read?" Reese nodded. "Good. Up South River, there should be a steamboat, the Cumberland that will be headin' north to Chesapeake Bay. It will be anchored there for several hours, takin' on passengers. Ask for Capt. Jones. Tell him you are 'free' and want to work your way north. Show him your papers. He'll take you on. Do your work, speak to no one, and keep out of sight as much as possible. If all goes well, when you land, don't arouse suspicion but try to find out where the main roads are to Baltimore. That's a big city near the head of the Bay."

"Excuse me, Mr. Carson, but where will I be when I get off the boat?"

"You'll be at the Port of Baltimore. Look for signs that say Philadelphia and follow the roads. On the outskirts of the city, ask someone for the Moore Farm. Show them your 'papers', if asked.

Go to the Moore's and tell them you need help gettin' up to New York. Nice black folks, the Moore's. They'll get you to Pennsylvania and tell you who to look for."

Reese remembered some of the signs he saw when he was transported by the two slave hunters. "I think I'll recognize some of the roads," he said hopefully.

"That's fine. Move quickly and keep out of sight. Get to the Moore farm safely. Tell them right off, 'James sent me'." Carson gave him a change of clothing and a hearty supper. "Best figure on leavin' about three o'clock in the morning—reach the steamboat by dawn—see the captain real early, before he starts loadin' passengers. Get some rest."

Reese felt overwhelmed by what lay ahead.

With Carson's blessings ringing in his ears, Reese headed out through the woods. He tried to keep the shoreline in sight all the way. Every sound, every crackling of branches brought renewed fear. He sighed with relief when streamers of light slowly lit up the sky as the sun's rays broke through. At least now he could see where he was going. Making his way down to the river's edge, he scanned the horizon. Sure enough, he could see a ship in the not too far distance. He increased his pace, his heart beating wildly as he approached the man standing at the foot of the gangplank. "Captain, Sir, I'm lookin' for work."

"I'm not the captain. What kind of work? Do you have your 'free papers'?

Reese became flustered. He recalled what Carson told him. "I need to speak to Capt. Jones. James told me . . ."

"Just a minute," the man quickly responded. "I'll get the Captain."

Captain Jones, a crusty old sea-going man, had a gruff demeanor that frightened Reese. He bit his lip as Jones barked. "What kind of work can ya do, boy? I'll not be transportin' lazy louts on me ship. Where are ya from and how did ya get here?"

Well, thought Reese, I do believe the man's an Irishman. He

sounds like Mrs. O. I hope he is as kind. "My name is Reese. I was sent to see you by Mr. James Carson."

"Come on board, me lad. We'll find ya some place ta sleep and assign ya yer chores." He hustled Reese up the gangplank and down stairs to the crew's quarters. "Sleep in that corner bunk and come to me fer orders. Don't be getting' too friendly with anyone. Do ya understand?" Reese nodded. The Captain continued, "I'll not have much time to be talkin' ta ya so listen carefully. When we dock, wait until everyone's gone on his or her way. I assume that James told ya what ta do from that point on. Now, get somethin' ta eat in the galley . . . the kitchen, lad, the kitchen."

Going about his chores, Reese peeked around corners and through doorways at the passengers. He had never seen people dressed so elegantly—the men suited and with high hats and the ladies in fine dresses, with their parasols, as they walked the deck. They appeared so carefree and happy. How different from the people in Five Points. The whole experience seemed unreal. How little he knew of the world outside of the poverty of the New York docks. If he got back to Mrs. O's safely, he was determined he would do something with his life.

With help from some Negroes in the neighborhood near the Baltimore docks, Reese found his way to the Moore farm. At the mention of James' name, the family welcomed him. The Moore's liked him. "Would y'all want to stay and work for us? We are lookin' for a hired hand."

"I thank you kindly but I am anxious to get back to New York." He explained his situation with Mrs. O'Rourke and the McCullough's. "They are my family and I love them."

During supper, they discussed the route they would follow into Pennsylvania. Quakers had a school and community enclave there. They would give him shelter after Mr. Moore dropped him off. Reese now understood how his mother had been able to reach New York. Still, quite a feat for a young, frightened runaway slave with a child.

The next morning, the Moore's loaded a wagon with sacks of grain and farm products. "We are goin' to follow my usual route of customers," Mr. Moore explained. "If anyone asks, y'all are our hired hand. Just keep calm. Every stop, follow my lead. I'll tell y'all what items to carry for the customer. Then, get back in the wagon and wait 'till I finish the transaction."

Reese mopped his brow.

Mrs. Moore assured him. "Don't worry. Y'all will do just fine."

For a good part of the day, they made several stops, without incident. As dusk approached, Mr. Moore reigned in the horses at a roadside eatery. "We are not too far from the Pennsylvania state line. I'll go get us something to eat. Lay low here in the wagon."

As Mr. Moore waited for his order, two men entered. They straddled stools and pounded on the counter, demanding service in loud, rough voices. The only waitress on duty called, "I'll be right with y'all."

Out in the wagon, Reese had turned his head and ducked down behind some bags of grain when he noticed the two men walking in his direction. He could not see them clearly but when he recognized their raucous voices, there was no mistaking who they were. "My God, it's Fred and Tom, the slave catchers," he whispered.

Inside the eatery, the two men became more and more abusive. When one of them slapped the waitress on the buttocks, Mr. Moore went to her defense. "Y'all lookin' for trouble. Keep your hands where they belong."

The larger of the two turned to him. "What in hell y'all gonna do 'bout it?"

At that moment, the cook stepped out of the kitchen with Mr. Moore's food and beverages. He placed them on the counter and faced the ruffians. "Git out! We don' serve white trash in here."

"What in hell y'all mean, nigger lover. We seen that nigger out in the wagon and y'all servin' this man here two meals. Is he about to eat both them plates of food . . . ?"

The cook reached under the counter and came up with a shotgun. "Y'all got thirty seconds to get outa here." He cocked the hammer.

Shouting profanities, the two men made a hasty retreat to their wagon. Within seconds, it disappeared from view. The sounds of their angry voices lingered in the air, gradually fading to silence.

Reese breathed a sigh of relief. When Mr. Moore returned, they sat up front together, eating. Reese told about his experience with Fred and Tom. "Sure did take a turn when I heard those voices."

"Well, not to worry none. We will be crossin' into Pennsylvania soon. Gotta getcha over to New Brighton to Quaker territory. It's miles out of the way and will take us the rest of the night. The Quakers are good folks—dead set against slavery."

Reese shook his head in disbelief. "I just can't believe so many white folks are willin' to help."

"It's a question of morality, son."

They arrived in New Brighton toward noon the next day. The Quakers welcomed them and one of the families, the Townsend's, brought them to their house where they immediately prepared a meal for the weary travelers.

After resting for a few hours, Mr. Moore hitched up the horses and was ready to leave. "God bless y'all, Reese. Get back to your loved ones safely." They shook hands.

"Thank you, thank you, sir. I'll be forever grateful to you." Reese felt sad as he watched Mr. Moore's wagon disappear from view. What a good man, he thought.

The Townsend's provided Reese with fresh clothing after a welcomed bath. He was then invited to join them at the hearth where, to his surprise, several other runaways were present. Mr. Townsend explained, "These men are sheltered here until we can get them on their way to Canada."

They spent several hours together exchanging stories and asking questions. One of the escaped slaves asked of his host, "Why are y'all willin' to put yo' lives in danger?"

"We believe the Fugitive Slave Bill is unjust. No escaped slave should have to be returned to his master. Slavery is wrong. All men are born free and equal."

Another interrupted, "Den why de marsuhs tell us we not free, dat dey owns us, we be deer slaves. Ah was bo'n on de plantation. Nobody done bought me, lak mah mammy an' pappy."

"That is what we are fightin' against," Mr. Townsend replied. "No human being should be sold or owned by anyone because that person was born on their property."

"Dey's offerin' rewards fo' slaves dat runs away. So many been brung back ta the marsuhs. Lucky if dey not beaten or worse. Some marsuhs real mean, some not."

Mr. Townsend continued. "We are goin' to petition—that means, to appeal—the Senate and the House of Representatives in Washington to do away with the Fugitive Slave Act. Meanwhile, we are keepin' the Underground Railroad as active as possible."

The balance of the evening continued in that vein. Reese was in awe that so many strangers would take such risks.

To the other runaways, Mr. Townsend advised, "Late tonight, you will be taken to Buttonwood. That is Arthur Bradford's home from which his son and a hired hand will travel with you to Ohio the next night. Then you will be taken to Canada by way of Niagara Falls. You, Reese, will travel with a trusted friend as far as Philadelphia where you will be dropped off at another safe house belonging to a free black man. He'll see that you get to a port in New Jersey. There you'll get on a barge that'll take you over to the New York docks. Now, the hour grows late. You'd all best go down to the cellar until I call you. Be ready to leave. Good luck."

Reese's head was spinning. He couldn't believe what was happening. His spirits soared as he lay down on a cot in the underground hideaway. Soon he would be back with his beloved Mrs. O and dear friends, the McCullough's. "Thank you, Lord," he said softly in the dark.

They arrived at the safe house on the outskirts of Philadelphia late the next night. He barely had time to thank the man and woman who brought him there. After introducing Reese to Jim Gardner, they wished him good luck and hastened away.

Jim was an elderly Negro. His broad smile displayed a set of white teeth, punctuated by an occasional missing tooth. "Welcome, welcome, son." He ushered Reese into the modest little house. "Make yo'self comfortable." The furnishings, though sparse, were cozy and inviting. Reese settled into a large armchair and sank into the colorful pillows. "I can't thank you enough. I hope this won't cause you any trouble."

"Don' 'spect no trouble. Pennsylvania's a Northern state. How come y'all talk so good—lak a white man?"

"I had some schoolin' on the farm where I live. My friend Sean sits with me everyday, teachin' me to read and write." Growing a little anxious, Reese asked, "How long before we go to the New Jersey shore?"

Jim laughed. "Jest be patient. Won't be long 'fore you be there. Jest hab dis bowl ob soup and git some sleep."

The next day, Reese awoke to the aroma of fried chittlin's and grits and strong coffee. Jim hollered, "Come on in hyah and git some ob dis food in yo' belly. Hyah's mah wife Cleo, mah son Reuben, and mah daughter Leona."

"Pleased to meet you." Reese smiled at them. Then he greedily consumed two large portions of food and a cup of coffee. Smacking his lips with pleasure, he told Cleo, "Sure is delicious, Mrs. Gardner."

"Son, call her Cleo, and me Jim."

When they finished eating, Reese asked, "How did you get up here, if you don't mind my askin' . . . were you ever a slave on a plantation? Or, were you born here . . . ?'"

Jim interrupted. "Mah mammy and pappy wuz slaves in Virginny, place near Danville, big plantations an' ah wuz bo'n dere. Ah remembers de cabins all built out ob logs an' dere wuz streets laid out between 'em. De chimbneys wuz built outta dirt an' sticks an' hit got terrible cold an' de snow piled up but de men wud pack dirt up under de house an' dat made it warm inside.

"Virginny is de bes' place for good eatin' an' good white folks.

Dey raised niggers tah sell an' dey kept dem in good condition. Didn't do no whippin' or mistreatin'. Once in a while Ol' Miss wud slap de cook's face an' tell her tuh bear 'round dere' or holler at de servin' boys tah git 'bout in a hurry." Jim slapped his thigh and laughed. "Sure did git them movin'!"

Reese cut in. "Did you run away? Did the Underground help you get here?"

"Well, ah did run away afta mah mammy died and pappy was sold. Dat wuz right afta de marsuh say he gwine ta sell some ob de orphans. So a few ob us ran away, hidin' out wid slaves on other plantations an' always worryin' 'bout outrunnin' them bloodhound nigger-dogs. Finally, we wuz helped by folks lak what helped y'all."

Reese listened, spellbound then asked, "Why did you settle here?"

"When ah found out ah cud work h'yah widout fear ob bein' sent back to the plantation, ah took mah chances. Did jest fine. Took me a wife, had chillun. Saved enough money to build dis house an' get a piece ob land."

"You've been here many years then?" Reese was fascinated by his story.

"'Cept when ah wuz tricked wun day. Slave catchers don' decoyed me, tuk me by riverboat back to Virginny. Ah was found guilty ob bein' a fugitive slave an' dey returned me to de plantation . . ."

Reese cut in, "I'm scared of that ever happenin' again to me—gettin' kidnapped and brought back to Maryland." He paused for a moment. "Sorry I interrupted you, Jim. How did you get back to your family?"

"Ya know, it's been many years now an' ah still cain't believe de wunnerful thing dey done, de white folk hyah in dis town . . . collected $500, came down to de plantation an' bought mah freedom. An', thank the good Lord, ah been hyah wid mah family ever since." He sighed. "Now, Reese, we best git an early start. Lak to git to New Jersey shore befo' dark. Git y'all on one ob dem barges goin' to the New York harbor. Y'all be all right afta dat?"

"Sure thing, Jim. Once I get back to the docks of New York City, I'm home."

CHAPTER IX

THERE WAS TURMOIL in Mrs. O's tenement when Mr. McIvey, who had made a special trip up to New York, told the landlady that Reese had escaped from Hampton Farm. "Jist as I was leavin' the place, a young man came runnin' out ta my wagon. 'Y'all don't worry none, mister. He's in good hands,' he told me. Then he ran off back ta the house. I'm sure he was tryin' ta tell me that Reese is all right."

Mrs. O wailed, "Oh, where is my Reese—cold and wet, no doubt, somewhere hidin' in woods, runnin' fer his life from them bounty hunters."

Maureen tried to calm her but, in truth, she was suffering the same fears. "The lad will be jist foine, you will see. He is probably makin' his way home, with the help of that underground everyone talks about."

"Reese wouldn't run away unless he had a plan or someone else had one for him," Sean chimed in.

This seemed to comfort Mrs. O. "Right ya are, and I tell ya now, when that boy comes home, I have plans fer all of us."

Those mysterious plans again, Maureen thought, but she said nothing.

The atmosphere in New York City grew increasingly tense as abolitionists clashed with pro-slavery factions. There were demonstrations in the streets and street corner speeches. Statements made by the President inflamed the situation. He held that even though he considered slavery an evil, he was determined to uphold Constitutional Law, which guaranteed Southern states the right to own their slaves.

President Buchanan denigrated the abolitionists claiming they were wrongfully instilling ideas of freedom and inciting the slaves to rebellion and murder. He contended that slavery was not a question of morality but one of Constitutional Law where the Southern states were concerned.

Much to Eamon's distress, while editors wrote impassioned words on the subject of abolition, Tammany Hall remained mute. The Party was still championing the tale that freeing the slaves would bring an influx into the City and would reduce the chances of immigrants getting any available jobs. This was a point of contention with the immigrants, already impoverished, and it created the anger and frustration that led to rioting, at times.

One day, while making his rounds, Eamon came upon a group of disgruntled men who were shouting at a Negro walking past them. "Go on with ya, get back to the plantation where ya belong. We don't need niggers takin' our jobs!" and with that, a couple of the men pounced upon the poor fellow. Eamon could not stand by and do nothing, so he yelled, "Stop that, ya fools. 'Tis ta the jail you all will be goin' fer hittin' a man who has done nothin' ta you." He attempted to pull them apart. At that moment, someone landed a bottle on the top of Eamon's head and he fell to the sidewalk.

Suddenly, whistles were heard as two policemen appeared on the scene. The assailants fled in all directions. Eamon lay on the ground. Witnesses verified that he had tried to help and was not guilty of any offense. The unfortunate Negro was trying to wipe his face of the blood which ran from his nose and a cut in his forehead. An ambulance arrived to take them to Mercy Hospital and the police concluded their questioning as to the attackers' identity. Both men were treated and released—Eamon looking the worst of the two.

When Eamon entered the apartment, his head in bandages, Maureen's shriek brought Sean running. "Oh, my God, Eamon, what have they done ta you? Where are the bastard eejits? They will get a good swift kick in the bollocks."

Sean was shocked at his mother's language but Eamon could not suppress the laugh that escaped his lips. It wasn't often that Maureen reverted to profanities and he hadn't seen her this angry in a long time. "Now, now, luv," he cajoled, "'tis only a bit of a scratch and 'twill pass soon enough."

She persisted. "Are you hurtin' much? Can I getcha somethin' ta drink, are you feelin' peckish? I made some bangers and mash. Will you eat somethin', darlin'?"

The last thing he wanted at that moment was food, but he answered, "Sweetheart, nothin' would be more pleasin' than ta have some supper with my family." He tried not to wince at the pain that racked his head for he knew Maureen would be frantic. I have dealt with much more than this, he thought. All I need is a bit of rest.

Sean studied his father's face. He could tell he was in pain, in spite of the valiant effort to hide it. "Mam, why don't you sleep in my bed tonight and I'll stay with Da. If he needs anything, I'll take care of it. You get some rest." Maureen reluctantly consented.

Eamon tossed and moaned all night and Sean could not sleep for fear of something terrible happening. He wondered what drove men to such low levels—to attack innocent people. In school, the problem of slavery was often discussed, but Sean was aware that even there, discretion was exercised. It was the trouble on the streets that worried him.

The next morning, Sean brought his father a cup of tea and a biscuit. "Don't get out of bed, Da. Just sit up a bit and have some breakfast. How do you feel?"

"Not so good, Sean. 'Tis the pain at the top of me head that will not go away. Do not say a word ta your mam. I do not want her worryin'."

Sean looked into his father's pale face so etched with pain. "Da, maybe we'd best go to hospital for another look-see. I know you are hurtin' bad. Please, Da."

When Eamon finished eating, Sean turned to put the dishes

in the sink. As he looked back toward Eamon's bed, he saw his father crumple into a heap on the floor. The thud his body made woke Maureen out of a deep slumber. She jumped out of bed and ran to Eamon's side. "Oh, Jaysus, Oh, God! Eamon, what is it? Oh, speak ta me, luv." She looked up at Sean; tears ran in rivulets down her cheeks. "Oh, son, go tell Mrs. O ta call a doctor. Hurry!" She sat there holding her husband in her arms, swaying to and fro, moaning and beseeching "Sweet Jesus" to help.

Mrs. O hastened into the room, with Sean following close at her heels. "Dr. Morgan will be here in no time at all, darlin'. Jist be calm." She glanced at Eamon, who lay still, and stifled a sob.

The doctor arrived within several minutes. Luckily, he lived on the next street and was the community doctor. He was a dedicated man and chose to practice in that area where he felt he was needed most. "Let's have a look at you, Mr. McCullough. Sean, help me lift him onto the bed." It did not take long for the doctor to determine that Eamon's skull was fractured. "Now, there's nothing to get excited about, but I believe that Eamon would be best served in a hospital. There, he'll get nursing service day and night and the proper medication."

The ambulance delivered not only Eamon but also a weeping Maureen, Mrs. O and Sean. They refused to leave the hospital until Eamon was examined and a bed assigned to him. It broke Maureen's heart to leave him. They had never been apart one day, except for that horrible experience of hers on the road from Tanniwilly. She insisted on waiting for Eamon to regain consciousness, which he did in late afternoon. Mrs. O and Sean urged her to go home to get some rest. She finally agreed, saying, "We will be back first thing this evening, luv." She kissed him lightly on his forehead. He blinked his eyes in response.

Mrs. O had a troubled look on her face as they entered her apartment. She insisted that Maureen and Sean have a bite to eat with her. "Ya know," she said suddenly, "if I had not been such a procrastinator, all this trouble with Reese, and now with Eamon, would have been avoided."

Maureen was puzzled. "What do you mean?"

"Well, ya know how I have said many times that I have a plan. Well, damn, I do have a plan—a plan ta get us out of here, ta a better place ta live. Stupid old woman that I am, I waited too long. Well, I will not wait any longer. As soon as Eamon is well and my Reese is back, we are movin' out of here. I swear it!"

Sean was excited. "You mean we are movin' to another house?"

"Not jist another house, my boy, but a different place—ta the farm area outside the City limits where we will have a nice home and a bit of property. Of course, I am takin' it fer granted that the McCullough's will agree ta join me. Oh, 'twill be so grand. Clean, fresh air, land ta farm vegetables, and a garden full of beautiful flowers . . ."

Maureen asked, "How is this ta happen? It sounds like a dream. Is this fer real? Oh, we would be more than happy ta go ta such a place with you."

"It has been a dream of mine fer a long while and now it is time ta make the dream come true. I have saved money these many years ta have a decent home and a piece of land of my own, before I leave this world. Havin' ya with me makes it all the more wonderful. Ya are family ta me."

"How kind of you ta think of us like that. You are a foine, generous woman."

"Tish, tish, Maureen. Let's get ready ta visit Eamon later. I'll jist take a nap now and ya get some rest, too. Be ready at 5 o'clock. Off with ya."

In their own room, Maureen and Sean spoke about the plans, no longer mysterious. "Can you imagine, Sean, we will be movin' outa this overcrowded, filthy neighborhood ta a little farm! Oh, Da will be so glad. He is tired of poundin' the pavements fer Tammany. God willin', we will be plantin' and workin' the soil like we did back home only this time it will be so different. Oh, thank the Lord, our lot is improvin' and, what is more important,

Sean, we will be gettin' you outa Five Points. At last, Sweet Jesus, at last." She whispered the last six words.

They sprang to their feet when Mrs. O knocked at the door and shouted, "Five o'clock!"

CHAPTER X

WHEN EAMON WAS discharged from the hospital, Mrs. O arranged a homecoming party in the saloon downstairs. Toward the end of the evening, Reese suddenly appeared in the doorway. Signaling with his finger to his lips, he sneaked up behind Mrs. O and threw his arms around her. She pulled out of his embrace. When she realized who it was, she cried, "Oh, God love ya! Home at last, my boy! Everybody, 'tis my Reese!"

The McCullough's surrounded him. Sean shook his hand. "Good to have you back. I missed you. We all did. Are you all right? We have lots to talk about."

"Sure do, Sean, but not tonight. I jest want to enjoy bein' home . . . to believe that this is not a dream." His eyes glistened.

Sean quickly pulled him aside, changing the subject. "You will not believe all that has been goin' on and, best of all, there is such good news. Mrs. O is sellin' this property to one of those rich builders. There's lots of talk about tearin' down the shanties and old tenements."

"Mrs. O's sellin'?" What'll happen to us?

"Not to worry, Reese. She said something about a farm."

"A farm! Lord, she's talked about a farm for so long. I never paid it no mind . . . thought we'd never leave Five Points." He took a deep breath which became a sigh. "A farm." He shook his head in amazement.

"It's goin' to be grand." Sean said.

The next morning, Mrs. O summoned the McCullough's and Reese to breakfast. "Now, Reese, my boy, tell us all."

As Reese described his journey to freedom, the emotions of his listeners ran the gamut from outrage to gratitude.

"Well now," said Mrs. O, "the family is whole again and the future is lookin' mighty promisin'."

It all became a reality the day the official-looking man, with briefcase in hand, came to see Mrs. O. When he left, she hastened to the McCullough's. "Look here," she yelled. "'Tis done. Here's the deed ta our place in the Heights—and Eamon, if anything happens ta me, this paper says you and Maureen own the farm."

Eamon looked at his wife in disbelief. They both began to speak at the same time, their words falling over each other like dominoes as they tried to thank her.

Mrs. O dismissed them with a wave of her hand and a "Tish, tish, 'tis nothin'. I've said it ta ya a million times. We are family. Now, let's have no more of this."

Speechless, Maureen gave her benefactor a hug.

*   *   *

It was 1858, a year after the Supreme Court issued its shattering Dred Scott decision that slaves were property and property is protected under the Constitution. Abraham Lincoln was running for the U. S. Senate seat of Stephen A. Douglas.

As they sat and talked over tea one day, Eamon asked, "Maureen, did you see the headlines in the New York Herald today? They have laid the Atlantic cable ta Europe and now we are gettin' the news from abroad in no time. There is goin' ta be a big celebration in New York City."

"Well, that is a good thing but there is so much unrest on the streets. Women are marchin' demandin' the right ta vote. The anti-abolitionists are still clashin' with the abolitionists. There is a terrible division between the North and the South. I fear, things are getting' worse."

"You know, darlin', 'tis this business of the trouble over the slaves that has me worried." His face clouded. "I cannot understand how a land can be one of liberty and yet allow the existence of slavery. It cannot be. Surely, one must destroy the other. I am afraid there will be a conflict."

Maureen leaned over to kiss him. She thought of Sean but tried to be optimistic. "My dear, do not worry yourself. Things will turn around."

*   *   *

It was easy for them to settle into the large, cozy farmhouse with its corn-and-potato producing three acres. There was even a stream nearby where they could enjoy fishing. Fresh air and clean water was something to which they had never been privileged. They were overjoyed in the genteel life of Northern Manhattan and its bucolic atmosphere.

The old farmhouse had a gambrel roof that sloped over the front and rear porches. The lower walls were fieldstone; the upper walls, white clapboard. Only the front of the house was of brick. There was a kitchen, a parlor, three bedrooms on the ground floor, two others upstairs, and a small alcove that Mrs. O promptly announced would be suitable for her "office".

There was a large fireplace in the kitchen where food was prepared in iron cookware. The hearth was lined with bricks which, when heated, would serve as additional burners for spider skillets.

Mrs. O purchased several wing chairs, a loveseat, and a few small lamp tables for the parlor. Against the wall stood a folded card table for playing games, working on sewing projects, or reading together. "Aren't these chairs somethin'? Mrs. O asked. "'Twas a clever man who designed them so's the sides protect ya from drafts."

Maureen added, "I am thinkin' 'tis the foot warmers in front of the chairs that are me favorites." The remark got a laugh, especially from Eamon who often was the recipient, in bed, of her cold feet on his own.

The bedrooms were comfortably furnished with large four poster beds, writing desks complemented by straight back chairs and washstands. Mrs. O's bedroom and "office" were to the rear of the parlor. Maureen and Eamon had one large bedroom to the front; Sean, the other. Reese had a bedroom upstairs.

The only disappointment was the lack of an indoor bathroom. "So many homes have them these days," Mrs. O observed. "We're still goin' ta the old outhouse, albeit a nicer one. Well, maybe someday that'll come too."

That year, Eamon voted for the first time in the City elections for mayor. Fernando Wood, a Democrat, won and replaced Mayor Daniel F. Tiemann. The party was now referred to as the Mozart Hall Democrats and gatherings were held at Jackson Hall on Horatio Street, corner of Greenwich Avenue. Once in a while, Eamon would take the horse-drawn trolley into the City to attend a meeting. Going into the City to vote was a thrill for Eamon. 'Oh, 'tis a grand feelin' ta be a part of the democratic process, ta be free ta choose the man you have faith in." Pride and excitement were in his voice.

Maureen often wondered how Eamon felt about farming after all this time. "Eamon, do you miss bein' downtown workin' fer the party? You niver told me—how did Mr. Kelly take the news that you were leavin' your job at Tammany?"

"'Twas no trouble. He said he was sorry ta see me go but he wished me the best of luck. Told me the Party would always be there for us."

Under Eamon's direction, Sean and Reese planted and harvested the crops. They built a corn crib for storage and dug out a root cellar in which they kept vegetables, at a temperature of 50 degrees. Mrs. O bought a horse and wagon and every week the boys would traverse Kingsbridge Road valley on their way to the crossing at Spuyten Duyvil Creek. Then they would head downtown to sell their produce to the greengrocers along the way.

Every time the boys returned from a trip, they always had interesting tidbits of news. One day, Sean said, "You know, there is such excitement in the City these days. There is a St. Patrick's Cathedral now on Fifth Avenue and 50th Street, and you should see all the diggin' and plantin' on the streets from 59th to past 100th. They've torn down all the shanties and put a lot of people to work, especially Irish laborers, I hear. There's to be a large park— Central Park, they're callin' it—for people to walk about and enjoy the trees and grass, with plenty of room for children to play. Oh, Mam it is grand to behold!"

Amused by his enthusiasm as well as impressed by it, Maureen said, "Surely 'tis an amazin' time we live in."

As the farm flourished, so did their business. Soon, the boys developed a regular route. Week after week, they made their runs downtown and never ceased to be surprised at the rapid changes in the Metropolis: the development of a theater district in Union Square, the growth of large, elaborate hotels and ornate restaurants.

The family settled into a pleasant routine. The only source of worry was the ominous unrest they sensed as demonstrations on the streets became a common occurrence and newspaper headlines screamed of Southern secession.

Eamon tried to be optimistic when Sean recounted such happenings. He feared that his early concerns about the anti-abolitionists were proving to be valid. "Sean, I am thinkin' what they are sayin' about the Mayor, him bein' in favor of the South's position—that cannot be helpin' the sityation any." He hesitated saying too much because Maureen reacted with fear at the possibility of conflict. "Do not worry, darlin'," he would tell her, "the government will straighten it all out." He would swing her around and do a bit of a jig and that always made her smile.

*   *   *

As their wagon approached the crossing at the Creek, one morning, Sean and Reese heard cries for help. They brought the wagon to a halt at the side of the road, jumped down and ran toward the sounds of pleas coming from some underbrush. There they came upon a wagon stuck in a ditch; next to it, a man was lying on the ground. A young girl, crying profusely, knelt at his side. When she saw them, she begged, "Please, please help my father. Oh, God!"

Sean could not help but notice what a beauty she was. Cupid's arrow found its mark. He was smitten. As she continued to plead, Sean regained his composure, aware that he must have been staring at her. He bent down to the still figure on the ground, then reassured her. "He's breathing. He's all right." To Reese he said, "Let's get the wagon out. We'll push from behind and you, Miss, please take the horse's reins and when I say so, lead him straight ahead. Can you do that all right?"

"Yes, yes, thank you," she whimpered.

Sean and Reese, up to their ankles in water, struggled. Sean told the girl, "Now! Lead the horse!"

Finally, as the horse pulled and they pushed, the wagon was upright. The boys gently lifted the man from the ground and laid him down on a blanket in the wagon. "Now, Miss, let us get you home so you may call a doctor for your father. My name is Sean McCullough and this is my friend, Reese Gordon. And who might you be?"

"My name is Jessica and my father is Bernard Wahlberg."

"Pleased to meet you." Sean helped her up to her seat. "Reese will drive your wagon while you look to your father and I'll follow in mine."

Jessica wiped the tears from her face and nodded. They took their places and turned the wagons around. Within a short while, they pulled into a neat, little farm. Sean recognized the area and realized that they were not far from their own place. When the wagons came to a halt, he jumped down and rushed over to help Jessica dismount.

Reese teased, "I could have done that."

Jessica blushed.

They lifted Mr. Wahlberg with care and carried him into the house where a frenzied Mrs. Wahlberg fluttered about, wringing her hands and wailing. "*Gott in himmel!*" as her daughter tried to assure her that "Papa is all right". Jessica introduced her "saviors", explaining how Sean and Reese heard her screams and came to the rescue. Intermittent moans told them that Mr. Wahlberg was now regaining consciousness.

Jessica rushed to his side. "Papa, all you all right? We'll get Dr. Brownstein to come see you . . ."

"No, no. No doctor. I am fine. See, I can get up." Saying that, he struggled to sit up but, at once, fell back on the bed. "Maybe a little later. Now—no doctor. I just need to rest."

Mrs. Wahlberg insisted that the boys stay for dinner to show her appreciation. Sean knew they were already late for their deliveries but he consented without hesitation.

Reese did not object after he saw the expression on Sean's face as he looked at Jessica. I do believe, he thought, my friend has fallen in love. Then he wondered how their customers would feel about the late deliveries—and the folks at home, when they did not return at their usual hour. He debated whether or not he should say something but changed his mind when he saw Sean's eyes fixed on Jessica. He kept quiet.

The meal was enjoyable. The boys departed with blessings from Mrs. Wahlberg trailing them out the door. Reese turned the wagon eastward and headed for the City.

The only thought in Sean's head was how would be manage to see Jessica again.

Later that evening, Sean described the events of the day to Mrs. O and his parents, after explaining the reason for being late.

"That is a foine thing you boys did," Eamon said. "And I am glad you have met our neighbors . . . uh, the Wahlbergs, did you say? Sounds German, I b'lieve, like some of them names down in the old neighborhood."

"Oh, Da, they are such nice, friendly people. The mother served us delicious things to eat, so thankful was she."

Reese added, "The daughter's mighty pretty, too."

Maureen could not help but notice the flush that spread over her son's cheeks. When she heard Sean's next comment, she sensed that her son was feeling pangs of young love.

"Do you think, Mam, it would be proper to stop at the Wahlberg's now and then," he stuttered, "that is, to see how Mr. Wahlberg is feelin'?"

"'Tis a kind thought and a friendly one but you do not want ta be intrudin' on their privacy." Maureen noticed the crestfallen look on her son's face, so she quickly added, "But, 'twould be the Christian thing ta do. There is no harm in stoppin' by, I suppose, but jist this once, mind you."

Sean beamed. "Thank you, Mam. Reese and I will do that tomorrow on our way home from our deliveries. So you know, we will be a little late for supper and you are not to worry."

Eamon and Maureen exchanged glances.

The next day was a Friday, and after the boys delivered their orders, Sean was anxious to turn homeward. When they stopped at the Wahlberg's, they were greeted at the door by Mrs. Wahlberg. "Welcome, welcome, you are just in time for our Sabbath dinner. Morris, look who's here," she called out, as she ushered them into the dining room.

Mr. Wahlberg sat at the head of the table. Seeing the boys, he shouted, "Welcome, welcome!"

A demure, prettier than ever Jessica sat at his side. A lighted candelabra stood at the other end of the table.

"Go, Jessica, get two more settings so the boys can join us," her mother ordered.

"Yes, Mama."

"Please, no," Sean interrupted. "I thank you kindly but we are expected home for supper. We were anxious to know how Mr. Wahlberg was feelin'. We'd best be on our way."

Mr. Wahlberg rose from his chair and put his arms around the two of them. "I am indebted to you lads and will never forget it. If you ever need my help, I am here. Please."

His wife echoed his sentiments. Jessica smiled demurely.

"Thank you and good night. We'll be goin' on our way." Sean turned to look at Jessica. "I hope to see you all again soon." As his eyes lingered on her face, a blush spread to the roots of her hair.

At the supper table, Sean told of the visit to the Wahlberg's. His enthusiasm about Jessica as "the prettiest girl I have ever seen" made Maureen put on 'the long face', especially after Eamon's comments.

Eamon said, "Lightin' candles and talkin' about the Sabbath dinner on a Friday night . . . that means they are believers in the Hebrew faith. I have seen it many times when makin' me rounds for the Party in Five Points."

"They may be lovely people, Sean, but do not be gettin' any romantic ideas about Jessica. Their ways are not the same as ours," Maureen said.

Sean replied quickly, "Oh, Mam, I am not havin' romantic ideas." The flush on his face betrayed him.

Eamon tried to deflect the tension building in Maureen. "Come now, me luv, our son has been brought up in the Catholic faith and when 'tis toime ta think of love and marriage, he will find a good Catholic girl." He winked at Sean. "Meantime, me dear, he has ta have friends. There is no harm in it." He patted his wife playfully on the fanny.

As usual, she could not resist a smile at Eamon's shenanigans. "Oh, go on with you now!"

Sean sighed, relieved.

A week later, on a Sunday afternoon, when the McCullough's

returned from church, there was a knock at the door. On the threshold stood a beaming Mrs. Wahlberg, followed by her husband and daughter. She handed Maureen a large container. "Darling, I am Betty Wahlberg. This is my husband Morris who the boys saved, bless them, and this is my daughter Jessica."

Taken aback, Maureen stood unmoving until Eamon said, "Well, darlin', ask the Wahlberg's ta come in. We cannot have them standin' in the doorway like that."

"Oh, yes, fer sure. Please forgive my bad manners but 'tis surprised I am ta see you." Maureen placed the container on the sideboard.

"It's a delicious compote. I made it for you from the wonderful fruits we grow on our farm. I hope you enjoy it."

"Thank you kindly," Maureen answered.

They stood awkwardly for another moment and then Maureen suggested, "Let us go into the parlor. Can I offer you a glass of juice or a cup of tea?"

"A cup of tea would do nicely, if it's not too much trouble. Jessica will have some juice, thank you."

"No trouble." Maureen bustled off to the kitchen.

Sean sat down near Jessica. "Good day to you."

A radiant Jessica responded, "And to you, too."

The expression on their faces was not lost on Eamon or, for that matter, on the Wahlberg's.

When Maureen served the beverages, Betty exclaimed, "I am so happy that we have found such lovely neighbors."

No one was happier than the two young people who sat, side by side, experiencing the exquisite early pains of desire.

$$* \quad * \quad *$$

Harvesting and keeping the farm intact took all their time and energy but no one complained. Mrs. O was now "somewhere around 80 or so" and the family did not want her to be involved in any work. "Sit and enjoy the fruits of your labor" they would say. Eamon bought her an old oak rocker that Maureen upholstered with two handmade pillows. "Twill keep your bones from achin'," she told Mrs. O, "and your bottom from hurtin'." They enjoyed a good laugh.

However, Mrs. O insisted, "While I am preservin' my bones and my bottom, there is not reason in the world why I cannot keep the records for our business transactions. After all, I did pretty good with keepin' my accounts straight in the tenement. That's how we ended up here!"

Her suggestion was unanimously approved.

Maureen ran the household, doing the cooking, cleaning and sewing. Eamon handled the maintenance and repairs, as well as the planting, with the help of Sean and Reese. The tempo of their lives became fine-tuned. There were, at last, content. One thing, however, worried Maureen: Sean was not continuing his education.

One evening, when she and Eamon shared a pot of tea with Mrs. O, Maureen broached the subject. "You know, I am truly upset that Sean is not receivin' any further schoolin'. I am still fumin' over the fact that he was kept out of the N. Y. Free Academy because we were poor. I was talkin' to Mrs. Burke the other day when she stepped by ta pick up her order. She told me that there is an Academy of the Holy Infancy up on 131ˢᵗ Street where courses are given in preparation for higher learnin'. Run by Christian Brothers. Even teach Latin and Greek. A good idea for Sean to take classes there."

Caught totally off guard, Eamon sat quietly. Mrs. O, however, was quick to comment. "That is a fine idea! We can spare him a couple of hours a day. You are right, Maureen, he should be goin' ta school. He'll be an important man someday, I guarantee it."

Eamon wondered how Sean would take the news.

That night, after supper, he told his son of their decision. Sean was totally in awe. After the initial shock wore off, he asked, "How about my chores? I have to do my share. It'll be too hard on you and Reese."

"You are not ta worry about that," Maureen said. "We will manage while you are in school and, after classes, you will help. It is settled then. Your father will go ta the Academy and sign you up."

That night Sean could not fall asleep. Ideas rapidly took shape in his mind. His father had said that the school was on 131ˢᵗ Street. That meant that, on his way, he would pass the road to the Wahlberg farm. Of course, by morning, he was totally dedicated to the concept of higher learning.

He never mentioned it, but he stopped occasionally at the Wahlberg's whenever he was sent on errands to the Village. He never stayed too long on those visits, but long enough to recognize that Jessica shared his feelings. Sometimes they sat for a while on the porch watching an occasional raccoon or possum scamper by. Looking off into the distance, she often exclaimed, "How tall and beautiful the treetops look, mingling with the clouds." As winter approached, she commented sadly, "Look, Sean, how the trees shed their leaves and bare their branches, as if they must hide their beautiful coats until they can be restored by spring rains and warm sunshine."

"You will be a famous poet someday, Jessica." He looked at the sweet, sensitive girl snuggling close to him and his being flooded with longing. Realizing that discretion was the better part of passion, he resisted the urge to kiss her—especially with Betty at the window every few minutes.

After these brief visits, Betty would often remark, "A fine boy. He's smart. He'll be a somebody, you can be sure of it." When she observed the way her daughter's eyes lit up, she would say, tactfully, "Sweetheart, I think the world of Sean and his family, but remember that their ways are not the same as ours."

On October 16, 1859, John Brown's unsuccessful raid on the federal arsenal and armory at Harper's Ferry, Virginia, was to become the spearhead of Southern rebellion. The purpose of the attack was to start a general slave insurrection by securing arms for them. John Brown's trial made all the headlines and became the marrow of speeches by presidential candidates for the upcoming 1860 election year. This topic soon became the hub of conversation around dinner tables.

On their rides to the City, Sean and Reese often spoke of the Harper Ferry incident. "Can you imagine, Reese, the courage of that man, leadin' an army of sixteen whites and five Negroes. Da says Brown wasn't expectin' a counter attack and was sure he'd be successful by capturing all the guns in the arsenal. But, they did not know that there was another building containing arms which the villagers got hold of. They stood with the militia men against the invaders."

"I don't understand why he couldn't get more Negroes to join him," Reese said.

"Probably because many of the freed slaves were afraid they would be riskin' their freedom."

"It's jest as well, I guess," Reese answered. "Maybe more would have died."

"Most of Brown's men died on the spot and the others will go on trial with him." Sean shook his head. "It seems that people are always dyin' for a dream that turns into a nightmare."

"Sean, do you expect there'll be a fight between the North and South?"

"Da says there's a good chance there'll be trouble between the anti-slavers and the slaveholders. Mam is already prayin' to all her saints for a peaceful end to the problem. I know she wouldn't approve of my goin' to fight, if it came to that."

"Sean, if there's fightin' to do, don't think I'd turn my back on it. I know there'll be hell to pay with Mrs. O, if I ever express myself that way. Sure is somethin' to think about, though."

They appraised each other briefly.

On December 2, 1859, in a courthouse in Charles Town, after a three-day trial, Judge Richard Parker sentenced John Brown to be hanged. One of the militia men guarding the site was John Wilkes Booth.

CHAPTER XI

CHRISTMAS OF 1859 was a pleasurable one for the McCullough's and the Wahlberg's. Mrs. O and Maureen prepared a lavish dinner of special cuts of meat they had cured in their smokehouse for this occasion. Their homegrown vegetables and another generous donation of fresh fruit compote from Betty rounded off the meal. The huge, open-faced apple pie and Christmas cookies sprinkled with nuts and candies that Mrs. O had baked were displayed on the sideboard, on a doily-lined pewter platter, decorated with sprigs of mint leaves.

When they were all seated around the large, oak table, Eamon said, "Let us say grace." All heads bowed. Maureen worried that the Wahlberg's might find certain foods objectionable but when she mentioned it to Betty, her response was, "Darling, in *your* house, we eat anything!"

Sean and Reese were in charge of setting the table and clearing, in between courses, so there was an uninterrupted ebb and flow of plates filled with food. "Good food and good company," said Sean, "is an unbeatable combination."

"Hear, hear," they all echoed.

Just before dessert, Eamon lifted his glass and the others followed suit. "I shall now recite me favorite blessing."

> May there always be work fer your hands ta do,
> May yer purse always hold a coin or two;
> May a rainbow be certain ta follow each rain;

May the hand of a friend always be near you;
May God fill your heart with gladness ta cheer you.

"Amen!" Bernard shouted. "May the good Lord always cause his countenance to shine upon you!"

The evening went well. The women got along famously, exchanging little bits of culinary and other homemaking anecdotes. Sean, Reese, and Jessica soon formed their own clique and left their elders to discuss the issues of the day.

Betty couldn't help commenting on Maureen's frock. "What a lovely dress you're wearing, my dear. I haven't seen anything like it around here or in the catalogues . . ."

"That is because I made it meself. I have always made me own wardrobe. I love ta sew."

Betty was animated. "Maureen, I hope you won't take this the wrong way, but would you consider sewing professionally—you know, for other ladies? I would be your best customer." She laughed and squeezed Maureen's hand.

"Oh, I would not know how ta handle that sort of sityation—bein' paid ta sew . . ."

"Don't you worry about that. I know some of my friends would give you lots of business."

Mrs. O chimed in. "I think it's a grand idea. Maureen, leave the figurin' out ta me, as far as chargin' goes."

"But what about the toime? I do not have . . ."

Mrs. O cut her short. "Shush now. We've got lots of help from the boys and Eamon. I'm still a good hand in the kitchen. There'll be plenty of time for ya, so what are ya hesitatin' for?"

"It's settled then," Betty said. "I'll bring the ladies here right after the New Year and you can talk style and fabric and price."

Maureen was speechless. She had dreamed of being a dressmaker back in the Old Country and now, suddenly, the opportunity was presenting itself. "Thank you, Betty. I do not know what ta say. I only hope I do not disappoint you or your friends."

The excited voices of the women attracted the attention of

Eamon and Bernard, who had been engrossed in a serious conversation about civil unrest. Eamon called across the room, "What are you all so excited about?"

At that point, Sean, Reese, and Jessica turned to listen.

"Well," Mrs. O said, "Betty here is goin' ta make a dressmaker out of our Maureen." She quickly explained the plan to them.

Eamon sat back, amazed. How fast changes had altered their lives from their leaving Five Points to live in the country and Sean going back to school, and now this opportunity for Maureen. He blinked his eyes. Yes, 'tis real. Turning to his wife, he asked, "So, luv, are you thinkin' you will be goin' into business soon?" He cast her one of his broad winks.

Maureen turned to Betty. I am surely grateful ta you fer all you are tryin' ta do. I will be thinkin' about it fer a bit. 'Tis a big decision. Can it hold until after the holidays?"

"Of course, darling. Whatever you decide. We are good friends, no matter what. Right?" She enveloped Maureen in a bear hug.

"Fer sure."

The rest of the evening was spent in pleasant conversation about the growth of the area and their neighbors and the expansion of the City itself. Before long, talk reverted to concerns about the unrest that hung like a "sword of Damocles" over the country.

Sean commented, "I hear that the Lincoln's come into the City often and stay at that fancy hotel, the Astor House."

"Yes, that's true," Bernard said. "A couple of men I do business with told me Mr. Lincoln is friendly with that famous Tribune editor, Horace Greeley. They have had some lively discussions, they tell me."

Eamon felt pangs of jealousy because he was not in a position to deal with businessmen the way Bernard was. He knew the Wahlberg's had connections in the Old Country with import/export firms. Bernard had told him about it and of his office in Manhattan, near Union Square.

"You have told me of the foine people you deal with," Eamon said. "It must be excitin' ta be in the City now and then."

"Well, Eamon, you must join me one of these days . . . spend an afternoon. I'll show you the ropes." He laughed.

"Thank you kindly, Bernard, but I am not sure I will find a day ta be away from the farm, but if I do, I can take you down ta Tammany Hall and introduce you ta some of the boys."

"Eamon, just say the word."

Maureen suggested, "I do b'lieve 'tis toime fer our tea."

"And for more of that wonderful pie and cookies," Sean added.

It soon grew late and the Wahlberg's said they would take their leave. Jessica seemed to be glued to her seat next to Sean's. Betty thought, the girl is entranced, as she called to her, "Jessica, dear, time to leave."

The girl jumped up with a start. "Oh, I'm sorry, Mama . . . Papa . . . I didn't . . ." She stopped, flustered, looking from her parents to the McCullough's to Sean, who was now equally flustered.

Bernard loved his daughter dearly and did not wish to cause her further embarrassment. "Come, sweetheart, you are tired. Let's go home so our good hosts can get some rest, too." As they were leaving, Bernard said, "*Shalom*, everybody. That means 'peace'. May we have the pleasure of your company soon."

CHAPTER XII

*T*HERE WAS NO *denying that New York was the entertainment city. Broadway, between Seventh and 13ᵗʰ Streets, became the theater district after dark when energies turned from merchandising to welcoming well-dressed patrons whose stylish carriages drew up to theaters and music halls.*

When Amos Emo built his Fifth Avenue Hotel on Madison and 23ʳᵈ Street, newspaper headlines called him a fool for venturing so far uptown. Now droves of visitors to the great metropolis flocked there.

Life on the Bowery took another turn. Although the street ran parallel to Broadway, no fancy carriages pulled up in front of its beer gardens, whorehouses, pawnbroker shops or two-bit flophouses. However, risqué shows drew patrons of all sorts.

On February 27, 1860, the new Cooper Institute in Manhattan welcomed the fifty-one year old Abraham Lincoln to speak to the Republicans of New York. Fifteen hundred people paid twenty-five cents each to listen to the "Westerner".

"You've no idea how things are changin'. It's amazin' down near City Hall at Park Row, they are now callin' the area 'newspaper row', what with some of the country's leading papers bein' published there—like the Tribune and the New York Times."

Always curious about City Hall, Eamon said, "I often wish I had some toime ta go downtown ta see the boys."

"Now, luv," Maureen suggested, "you can go in some day with Sean, if you like."

"Maybe so, maybe so." But, Eamon did not believe it for one minute.

On the evening of February 27, 1860, Sean returned from the City later than usual. He saw that his mother was upset. "I am late, Mam, but I have amazin' news. When I made the delivery to Mr. Donaldson, the greengrocer on Astor Place, he told me that Mr. Lincoln was to speak at Cooper Institute this very night. You should have seen the excitement on the streets. People everywhere talkin' about him and his runnin' for President."

"So what are you tellin' me? You are late because you were observin' people on the street? And me here worryin' meself sick!"

"Mam, please listen. I parked the wagon on a side street and walked to the entrance of Cooper Institute hopin' I might catch a glimpse of the great man. I only intended to stay a couple of minutes. Well," he inhaled deeply, "you won't believe what happened next." His voice rose. "A carriage pulls up and as the driver gets down to unload his passenger, up rears the horse on its hind legs, whinnying, forelegs thrashin'. Everyone's screamin' . . . the carriage is tippin' to one side . . ." He paused.

"Yes, yes, so what then?" Eamon pressed.

"Well, I don't know what possessed me, but I jump up onto the driver's seat as fast as I can grabbin' the reins while I try to steady the darn horse. He just keeps rearin' up and kickin'. Everyone's still screamin'. By now, I'm yellin' to the creature and tuggin' as hard as I can. Finally, with one last pull and a shout, I'm able to bring the horse down on all fours. Now, he's standin' calmly and snortin' like a steam engine."

Maureen gasped. "My God, Sean, you could have been killed!"

Eamon urged Sean, "Go on, go on."

"Give the boy a chance to catch his breath," Mrs. O admonished.

"You should have been there. Everybody started applaudin' and callin' me a hero. When I climb down, the next thing I know, the gentleman in the carriage gets out. His hand reached out for mine. He wants to thank me, I'm thinkin'. People around us are clappin' harder and louder. Lookin' more closely at the man, I realize the clappin' is not for me but for the man whose hand I'm shakin'. Then I hear a voice I'll never forget.

'You are a courageous lad and I shall always be grateful to you. What is your name?'

I can barely answer. "Sean, Sean McCullough, Mr. Lincoln, Sir".

A loud gasp and a chorus of "Oh, my God!" halted Sean's narrative.

Reese was in awe. "You really shook the man's hand?"

"Wait," Sean continued, "the best is yet to come. Mr. Lincoln asks me about myself—do I live in Manhattan. I tell him I don't and explain that I stopped by hopin' to get a glimpse of the man who would be runnin' for President, and he says, 'Would you be my guest and take a seat up close to listen to what I have to say?'"

More gasps as Sean continued. "I had trouble gettin' my wits together. Swallowin' hard, I manage a nod. 'Take this fine lad to a front row seat' he tells the usher at the door. There's lots more clappin' again as I walk just behind Mr. Lincoln into the buildin'.

"Mr. Lincoln is such a wonderful speaker. I was sittin' on the edge of my seat the whole time. Then when he finishes talkin', he takes his bows and says 'God bless us all' and goes to the end of the platform where he signals to me. 'Son, I hope you enjoyed my speech and understand what I am trying to do.' I assure him that I and my family are in full support. That brought a smile to his face.

"I realize how late it must be gettin' so I bid him goodnight and he thanks me again and says, 'My little friend, I am at your call, if you ever wish to speak to me.' We shake hands again. I tell you, my heart was in my mouth!"

Mrs. O, ever the political animal, observed, "'Tis a fortunate meetin', fer sure. Influence in high places never hurt anyone." She laughed heartily. "Ya done well, Sean."

At that moment, "influence in high places" was furthest from his mind. He could hardly wait to tell Jessica about his wonderful experience. Tomorrow, he hoped, after his classes.

"All right, Mr. Hero, 'tis off ta bed with you." Maureen

interrupted his reverie. "Tomorrow morning will be here only too soon and you have ta be awake fer your classes."

Sean kissed his parents, said goodnight to all and went to his room, his mind still racing.

Maureen watched him go and then turned to the others, "That boy will be a great man someday." Her face flushed with pride.

"Ya got that right," Mrs. O agreed.

They sat quietly for a moment, digesting the details of Sean's adventure. Then Maureen suggested, "Well, 'tis toime we all retired. There is lots of work ta be done around here and Sean's shakin' the hand of Mr. Lincoln will not change that. So, I bid you goodnight."

Sean awoke intermittently, through the night, squinting at the window, searching for telltale rays of morning light. His meeting with Abraham Lincoln and the anticipation of visiting Jessica left him virtually sleepless.

In class, at the Academy, he sat in his seat as though he were on hot coals. Brother McIntyre noticed Sean's fidgeting. "Are you not feeling well today, my boy? You seem unable to sit still for a minute."

"Oh, Brother McIntyre, I am sorry if I disturb the class but I've something on my mind that I would like to talk about . . . something that happened to me in Manhattan."

Not knowing what to expect from the mouth of a seventeen year old, the Brother answered hesitantly, "Now, son, perhaps you should tell me . . . uh, privately."

Sean laughed. "Brother, I am not going to speak about anything improper, if that's what you're thinkin'. It's about Mr. Lincoln . . . I met Mr. Lincoln last night! Can you believe that? I still can't."

Surprised, the teacher asked, "How on earth did you manage that?"

Sean recounted the events to his astonished listeners. After class, as Sean rushed out of the building, the other boys cleared a path for him, bowing in deference to the "famous one".

It was a week since he had last seen Jessica. How he missed

her! True, she had come to the house with her mother when Betty brought her club ladies to see Maureen about sewing up some frocks, but Jessica was obliged to stay with them. All he could manage was a brief glance as he went about his chores. He quickened the horse's pace as he hastened to the Wahlberg farm.

Betty, always glad to see him, ushered him into the sitting room and called, loudly, "Look, Papa, Sean is here to visit." Even though she suspected why Sean really came, she perpetuated the illusion that his visits were to the family.

Morris came into the sitting room. "Good to see you, Sean. How are your folks?" He shook his hand warmly.

"Everyone's fine, Mr. Wahlberg." Sean looked around nervously. "Is Jessica home? I have some great news."

The Wahlberg's exchanged glances. They were not unaware of the close relationship developing and had discussed the situation many times, with and without Jessica. "I'll go fetch her," Betty said. "I'm sure she will want to hear your news."

While they enjoyed a cup of tea and Betty's always delicious cakes, Sean related the events of the previous evening. The reaction he got was the same as it had been at home. Amazement! When they finished plying him with questions, Sean asked, "Is it all right if Jessica and I go for a walk? We won't be long. I have to be gettin' back to my responsibilities." He looked from Betty to Morris.

"Of course, go."

As Betty watched them walk down the path, out of sight, she sighed. "Such a lovely boy, Morris. I love him like a son. But—for Jessica—how could this ever work? He's Irish-Catholic and we're Jewish. Morris, this is breaking my heart. You see how they look at each other."

"Please, Betty, no one has said anything serious. They are good friends, that's all. He's a fine boy with a good upbringing and I am sure, when it is time to pick, he will choose a young lady with the same background as his."

"What are you talking 'background'? Love doesn't know from background. Just look at their faces when they are together. Mark my words, the children are in love."

Morris kept his thoughts to himself. He dismissed her last statement with a wave of his hand.

Jessica and Sean walked together, hand in hand. The slowly descending sun lent vitality to their bodies as the clean, invigorating fresh air filled their lungs. "Look, Sean, how the sun hangs like a bright chandelier shedding its light over everything. But not for long. Soon it will set, casting beautiful shadows on the fields and colorful streamers across the sky. How I love this time of day!"

He looked at her adoringly. "And I love the way you have with words, Jessica." Then he added simply and softly, "And I love you." He squeezed her hand.

His last three words stopped her in her tracks. Sean just expressed the feelings she carried for so long in her heart. Turning to him, she took both his hands in hers and whispered, "I love you, too, Sean—forever."

He kissed her quickly on the lips and held her close, his heart pounding. Closing his eyes, he inhaled the fragrance of her beautiful hair. At that moment, Sean wanted to shout out how much he loved her, but he said, softly, "Jessica, you have made me a happy man." He added, soberly, "Do you think your mother and father will be in favor of us lovin' each other?"

"What about your parents? Will they accept *me*? I know our families are good friends but . . ."

Sean interrupted. "Now, my sweet girl, let's not worry about that. We have too much to be happy about. We are in love!" He kissed her again, hungrily and longingly. Quickly regaining his composure, he said, 'Now, darlin', we've got to go back so I can get home before it grows late. I don't want Mam upset with me."

He looked into her troubled face. "Don't worry, luv. I'll talk to Mam about us. Don't say anything to your parents yet. Remember, I love you for always. That will never change. You are not to worry. It will all be grand, I promise you." He turned her face to his and kissed her lightly on the tip of her nose and then on the lips. "Now, my dearest, I must go."

They turned back onto the path leading to the house. Betty was at her usual post, peeking from a corner of the front window. She observed them carefully; saw how Sean leaned over to whisper in her daughter's ear; saw the reaction on Jessica's face. "Something has changed," she said aloud.

As Jessica approached the front door, Betty quickly withdrew to the kitchen. As she entered the house, she called, "Mama!"

Betty came out of the kitchen. "Yes, darling?"

"I'm going upstairs to wash and change. I'll help you get dinner ready in a few minutes."

"Fine, darling." She watched her daughter practically float up the stairs, her feet barely touching the steps.

"*Oy vey!*" Betty muttered as she went in search of her husband.

*   *   *

As Eamon came through the door, he heard Maureen shouting. "Saints preserve us, are you daft?" At first, he though she was directing the words at him until he saw Sean cowering in a corner of the kitchen. "What is happenin'? What is it? he asked.

Maureen's piercing voice continued. "I told you 'twould be trouble. I knew no good could come of it . . . jist trouble . . . trouble fer all of us."

"Wife, why are you carryin' on so?" He turned to Sean. "What has happened to bother your mother so?"

"Oh, Da, I've just been tellin' Mam that Jessica and I . . . well, we've declared our love for each other."

"What!" Eamon exploded. He looked from his son to his wife. 'Twill do no good ta join the shoutin' he decided, regaining his composure. "Now, Maureen, darlin' . . . Sean . . . let us sit down and discuss this like intelligent people. But first, dear wife, how about a good, strong cup of tea fer us?" He looked at her, pleadingly, realizing that he should have seen this coming: the two of them always edgin' toward each other and whisperin'. He ran his fingers through his hair and took a deep breath.

"Now, Sean boy, are you not considerin' the differences between you . . . in your beliefs, your backgrounds? Sure, friendship is foine in spite of things like that but . . ."

"Da! We love each other. We don't care about 'differences'!" Sean bristled.

His outburst took his parents by surprise. Maureen wrung her hands. "Do you not see the trouble this will cause us with the Church? Oh, Lord, Father Ryan will surely have you excommunicated!" The cups of tea shook in her hands as she set them down on the table.

"I don't care about the Church or Father Ryan. Where was the Church when we were starvin'? 'Pay the landlord' they kept tellin' us while we had nothin' but rotten potatoes to eat."

"Do you dare show disrespect fer the Church . . . and fer me and your father?"

"Mam, I don't want to do that. I want you to understand how Jessica and I feel. I want you to be happy for us," Sean pleaded.

"Oh, Jaysus!" Maureen reached for her rosary. "Hail Mary, full of grace . . ."

Eamon put his arms around her. "Sweetheart, calm yourself. Let the boy have his say. He is sensible and Jessica is smart. 'Tis sure I am they will make the right decision."

Sean retorted, "The only decision we are interested in makin', we've already made!" He stormed out of the room. They heard his bedroom door slam.

The distraught parents sat in silence. Sean had never defied them before. They faced each other, unable to speak. A feeling of helplessness washed over them like a tidal wave, engulfing them, drowning them in misery. Maureen sobbed.

Mrs. O poked her head into the kitchen. "I heard every word and if ya don't mind an old woman offerin' a bit of advice . . . ?" She waited a second and sensing no opposition, she added, "I'd have a talk with the Wahlberg's. I believe ya'll find they are on the same side of the fence. Religion is just as important ta them. Think about it. Now I bid ya good night."

"Eamon," Maureen said, "we must go ta see them t'morra. There is no toime ta waste."

Long after Maureen fell asleep, Eamon sat in his reading chair. His mind flooded with memories. He recalled the objections of Maureen's family when he proposed marriage, him being a farmer and a Protestant, at that! That he might lose the love of his life, frightened him. Luckily, compromises had been agreed to. Eamon converted to Catholicism so they could be married in the Church and then rented a piece of land not too far out of the city, so Maureen could be near her parents. He drew a deep breath and wondered if there was any possibility for compromise in his son's situation. His heart ached for Sean.

*   *   *

The McCullough's and the Wahlberg's sat awkwardly facing each other in the parlor. Their sober expressions bespoke a multitude of words. Eamon, trying to be as diplomatic as possible, had just announced their concerns about Sean and Jessica. "You know how much we love your daughter. You are like family, but you must understand, we are devout Catholics and 'tis not acceptable ta the Church ta choose a partner of another faith." He lowered his eyes and shifted his feet.

Betty spoke up. "Eamon, my dear, we understand perfectly. We feel the same way. Mixed marriage has always been a big issue in our faith, too. I mean, it is something almost unheard of . . ." Her voice trailed off. Jessica's inconsolable sobbing still echoed in her ears.

"Well," Maureen said firmly, "we jist hafta end it now, do we not? We are askin' Father Ryan ta come see Sean. He will be talkin' some sense into him, fer sure." She added, quickly, "Your daughter is a foine girl and dear ta us but . . . marriage, children . . ."

Morris interjected, "We understand. Maureen, Eamon, rest easy. We'll talk to Jessica. She is a good girl and will do what is right." After what seemed an endless silence, he rubbed his hands together and suggested, "Now, dear friends, let us have a cup of tea and some of Betty's special dessert."

They followed Morris, as Betty beckoned them all into the kitchen.

CHAPTER XIII

*A*BRAHAM LINCOLN WAS elected President in 1860. In spite of the warnings that secession could occur, he never contemplated the possibility of the government disintegrating. While campaigning, he had challenged Stephen A. Douglas to debates on the issue of slavery. Douglas sponsored the Kansas-Nebraska bill advocating that people must decide for themselves whether or not they wanted slavery. This bill created bedlam. Lincoln, with great passion and moral outrage, argued that slavery must not be allowed to spread, that it was a "reprehensible institution which we cannot endure:. In spite of his attempts to assuage the South with promises that he would not interfere with their way of life, within ninety days of his election, seven states threatened to secede.

In 1861, during the second year of his Presidency, paper money was introduced, coins were minted in gold, silver or copper—and the Civil War began.

On April 15th, the President issued a proclamation calling forth "the militia of the several States of the Union, to the aggregate number of 75,000 . . ." He appealed to "all loyal citizens to favor, facilitate and aid this effort to maintain the honor, the integrity and the existence of our National Union . . ." All newspapers carried the proclamation in its entirety.

As the McCullough's sat around the dinner table, Sean read President Lincoln's proclamation aloud. When he finished he was in a feverish state. "Oh, Mam, Da—the President is askin' for our help. You know, he needs men to defend the principles of freedom."

Maureen interrupted. "Listen to me, Sean, the President is not talkin' about young boys like yourself who are needed at home. There are plenty of men in the militia, I am sure." She looked anxiously at Eamon to say something.

Eamon could not bear the thought of his son going off to war. "Sean, you are needed here and you need ta get your edycation ta make somethin' of yourself. You know, we went through a lot ta come ta this country, mostly for you ta be free and have a chance ta be somebody."

"That is exactly the point, Da. We've got to help the land that's givin' us this opportunity."

Maureen ran from the room.

"Oh, Jaysus, now see what you have done—you have upset your mother!" Eamon snapped. With that, he left to find Maureen.

Sean sat alone. Tears spilled over as he lowered his head onto his folded arms. Everything seemed to be going wrong. He loved Jessica and wanted to marry her. His parents were irate and worried about ex-communication. Now, he upset them again by expressing his desire to serve in the Union Army.

In bed, Sean tossed and thrashed about most of the night. "Oh, Sweet Jesus," he whispered softly in the dark, "I'm doin' nothin' but breakin' the hearts of my loved ones." Finally, he dozed off, with a prayer lingering on his lips.

Both families persisted in their remonstrations. Sean and Jessica were not permitted to spend any time alone and only saw each other when the families had tea together. These social meetings soon dwindled. The frustration of the young lovers increased.

When Sean broached the subject to his mother, she remained firm. "How can you consider joinin' forever with someone who is not a Catholic? Are you not thinkin' of the salvation of your soul?"

"Mam, I want to think about my life here on earth and spendin' it with someone I truly love and who loves me."

"Sean, the Lord would not pardon such a sin . . . and what about children. They should grow up seein' both parents prayin' the same way, goin' ta confession and Holy Communion together. You know, 'tis the mother who teaches the children how ta pray. What would Jessica be teachin' your offspring? She could not even teach them ta make the Sign of the Cross. Oh, Lord!" Maureen wailed.

"Mam, I've done a lot of thinkin'. America is the land of the free, is it not? That's what you and Da have always taught me. Then why can't I be free to choose the person to share my life? I'm not sayin' that it's the best way when there's a difference of religion, but I believe that shouldn't stop two people in love."

"Oh, dear Jesus, I thought we taught you ta be a devoted son of the Church. Sean, listen ta me. Your life will become one of compromise. What will happen ta your spiritual life—the salvation of your soul?"

"I'll leave that for God to decide. Mam, I believe more and more that if people would only try to understand each other, the world would be a better place."

"Sean, even Mr. Wahlberg says that the scriptures strictly forbid Jews from marryin' out of the faith . . ."

"We don't care! Jessica and I want to be together and we will find a way . . ."

Maureen cut him off. "We have asked Father Ryan ta come by this evenin' ta have a talk with you."

"Mam, there's nothin' he can say that will change anything."

Maureen burst into tears.

As Sean rushed out of the room, he passed his father who had just come in from his chores. "Why are you rushin' so? I need you ta get the wagon ready and loaded fer the deliveries in the City tomorra."

"Da, go see Mam. She's upset again. I'm truly sorry."

"Oh, Lord, what have you said now?" All Eamon heard was the front door closing.

Sean and Jessica devised a plan for contacting each other. They left notes under a huge rock that sat down the road from the entrance to the Wahlberg farm. She often walked to the nearby woods where she would sit in a clearing, writing poetry. On her way, she would stop at the boulder, retrieve any messages and continue on to her "special place". Sean would join her there whenever he could.

This particular day, Sean was to meet her there. As she approached the large tree stump upon which she usually sat, she reminisced about the day Sean had asked her to marry him. She had somehow sensed that meeting would be different—something special—because Sean was excited; his demeanor was somewhat altered from the dour expression he had worn of late. He was animated, smiling, as he took her hand in his. Clearing his throat several times, he looked earnestly into her eyes. "Jessica, darlin', will you be my wife?" He kissed her swiftly on both cheeks and pressed her close to him.

She could still feel the emotion of her hot tears and pounding heart. It had been almost impossible for her to answer. Her breath caught in her throat. Inhaling sharply, she had almost shouted, "Yes, yes. I want nothing more but to spend my life with you!" Then, in a sober vein, she asked, "But, dear Sean, how will we ever . . . ?"

"Come here, my love, and I'll kiss away all your doubts and fears. Let's spend a happy hour together and when next we meet, I'll tell you more about my plans."

Jessica smiled as she recalled that day and now she waited nervously for Sean. It wasn't long before he appeared and they sat together underneath the huge, beautiful elm, whose branches spread wide over them like a canopy. She could hardly wait to hear about his "plans". These moments alone with him were precious to her. When they spoke of their future together, she believed it would be so.

Sean confided, "I've been savin' up some coin, as my father would say, and I've been watchin' for 'help wanted' signs in the City. There are many of those and I'm sure to get a job . . ."

"But, Sean," Jessica interrupted, "you've told me so many times that most signs say 'No Irish'. I'm afraid you'll have a hard time."

"Perhaps so, but not to worry, Sweetheart, I've another ace up my sleeve. Mr. Donaldson, the greengrocer on Astor Place, has often said he wished he had a lad like me to help him. So, maybe now's the time to put him to the test." He winked reassuringly. Jessica snuggled closer. "And," Sean added, "there are lots of places with rooms-to-let. We'll find a place to live, for sure."

The thought of what lay in store for them both frightened and excited Jessica, but, at the moment, just being together and so much in love was enough. They continued to speak about the future, words tumbling over each other. Finally, Sean took his leave, reminding her to look for a message within a day or two.

After Sean left, Jessica went back to the stump of the tree where she had left her notebook. Words flowed on paper, as she expressed her thoughts:

> Why can't people love each other, no matter
> What religion they believe?
> Why can't others understand, so there'd be
> No need to deceive?
> Sean is my love; he stands tall and strong
> Giving me strength and courage.
> My mother and father I do love
> As Sean does his.
> We hope and pray, their blessings
> They will give.

She sat quietly for a time, unaware that the long shadows forming across the meadow heralded the setting of the sun. Her reverie came to an abrupt end when she realized it was dusk. She mustn't worry her parents.

Two days later, Sean left a note asking her to meet him a little earlier than usual. "We're going into the City together, my love, so wear your Sunday best."

After his classes that morning, Sean came home and prepared

for his trip to Manhattan. He knew Reese would not be accompanying him because he had some repairs to do for Mrs. O. Maureen was curious. "Are you not changin' into your work clothes? You will be spoilin' your good pants and shirt."

"There's no time now if I'm to make all of today's deliveries. Don't worry, Mam, I'll be careful not to soil or tear anythin'." He laughed and kissed her. This was one day he wanted to look proper going into the City.

As Sean approached the clearing, his face clouded with doubt. Would Jessica be waiting? This was asking a lot of her—a big sacrifice—should he have done that? He was suddenly filled with apprehension. Well, if she wasn't there, he would understand and have to find another way. It was impossible to think of living without her. "Please let her be there," he prayed softly.

When Betty went up to Jessica's room to tell her lunch was ready, she found it vacant. The bed was made, as usual, and all her things were neatly in place, but where was Jessica? Then she noticed a sheet of paper propped up against a book on the desk. Betty reached for it with trembling hands. She was unable to stifle the scream that escaped her lips. It brought Morris running up the stairs.

"What? What is it? Betty, are you all right?"

"Oh, Morris, we have lost our Jessica," she sobbed, as she handed him the poem.

The opening in the woods was empty. Sean sat a while and then turned the wagon to leave. Suddenly, a breathless Jessica emerged from behind some trees. "I'm here, Sean, I'm here!"

His heart leapt for joy. As he helped her into the wagon, he kissed her again and again.

"Sean, could we just sit here a few minutes and talk. I'm all out of breath. There are some things I want to say, my darling."

"My beloved, my wife," Sean whispered and nuzzled her ear.

The lovers sat in the clearing for a long time. Sean grew uneasy. Jessica had so many questions. "What will we do in the City, Sean? Both our families are farm people and we've been raised to be the same."

Sean countered, "But, darlin', it seems to me with all this book learnin' I'm doin' at the Academy, I should be fit for somethin' a little finer, don't you think?"

"What I think is that someday you could be President, if you put your mind to it. But, right now . . ."

"I've got it all planned. After I work a while and save enough money, we'll move to Greenwich Village or maybe even Gramercy Park . . . oh, darlin', we'll be real city folk and have a grand life."

She winced and turned her head away. When she looked back at him, about to speak, he spoke instead. "I can see by the look of despair on your face that you've changed your mind. Oh, Jessica, why?"

She began to cry. "I can't do this. My parents will be heartbroken—devastated. I am their only child. Sean, don't you see what this will do to your parents, as well? Maybe we could talk to them . . . ?"

"No, Jessica. There's no more talkin'. Go home, my love. I know what I must do."

CHAPTER XIV

*D*IN AND EXCITEMENT *were characteristic of Manhattan. Everyone seemed to be in a hurry. Life was hectic. Everything was done with great anxiety. The leading thoroughfare was Broadway where the noise and clatter of thousands of horse drawn vehicles added to the confusion. In terms of the impending war between the states, it was a city wearing two hats: it housed the headquarters of the abolitionist press and was, at the same time, strongly "copperhead".*

Two anti-war Democrats, Mayor Fernando Wood and Samuel F. B. Morse (famous painter, developer of the code), led the battle against the Administration. Unable to continue telegraphic communications with the South, Morse shared the concerns of Northern industrialists, especially in New York, that they would lose important trade contracts. New York shipped almost as much cotton as New Orleans and Mobile and much of the clothing worn in the South was manufactured in New York City. Millions of dollars could be lost if the South reneged on its obligations.

Everywhere there was talk of war. Morse's worst fears were soon to be realized.

Sean steered the wagon along its customary route, past Cooper Institute where he had heard President Lincoln speak, to Astor Place and then to Greenwich Village and Washington Square. As he made his rounds, he noticed recruiting posters everywhere. One, in particular, caught his eye: *Young America and Old Ireland—one and inseparable—Irishmen to the field! strike a blow victoriously for*

Democracy and Liberty. Sean climbed down to read the small print. *Apply immediately to Col. Galligher, at the Headquarters of the Irish Dragoons, n.w. corner 7ᵗʰ and Chestnut Streets.* That's practically around the corner, Sean thought.

That night the destinies of two families took unexpected turns.

When Jessica returned to the farmhouse, the overjoyed Wahlberg's greeted her with open arms. Jessica, however, crying bitterly, explained all that had transpired. Betty and Morris kept alternating with, "That's all right, darling" and "Don't cry, sweetheart", until Jessica shouted, "It's not all right but I just couldn't do it!" With that, she ran to her room.

Her parents did not follow her. For the rest of the evening, they listened to her sobbing.

At the McCullough's, it was a similar scenario. When Sean returned from the City, he threw some papers down on the kitchen table.

"What is that?" Eamon asked.

"Those are my enlistment papers, Da. I'm goin' to the War."

Maureen and Mrs. O screamed, "No!" and Eamon's face filled with shock and fear. Reese glanced Sean's way but said nothing as he continued to serve their supper.

"Oh, Mother of Jesus, what have we done ta deserve this?" Maureen cried out. "How could you do such a thing without speakin' ta us? You know how we feel about this. Where is your respect fer your elders?"

Eamon asked, "Son, why would you fight ta free slaves that might be takin' jobs away from us? And, more important, you could be maimed or even killed . . ." He fell silent.

Frustrated and furious, Sean shouted, "If I can't be with Jessica then I'll be done with the lot of you. You made this happen. I hope you're satisfied!"

The desolate trio faced each other, speechless. Eamon stood up and as he turned away, he said quietly, "Sometimes we create our own hell. The Lord have mercy."

*   *   *

On April 12, 1861, in Charleston, at 4:30 a.m., Confederate soldiers opened fire on Fort Sumpter. Thus began the Civil War. A proclamation by President Lincoln, a little more than a month after his inauguration, called up "the militia of the several states of the Union . . . in order to cause the laws to be duly executed . . . . I appeal to all loyal citizens to favor, facilitate and aid this effort to maintain the honor, the integrity and the existence of our National Union . . . ."

In January 1861, Mayor Fernando Wood urged the secession of New York City to form the free city of Tri-insula. In April, 100,000 citizens, in a mass demonstration of loyalty to the Union, assembled at the statue of George Washington in Union Square.

The 1ˢᵗ regiment of the new "Irish Brigade", the 69ᵗʰ New York State Volunteers, was mustered into service and left New York for Washington, D.C. on November 18, 1861, to join the Army of the Potomac.

Sean was scheduled to leave with the 69ᵗʰ NYSV's. He wanted desperately to see Jessica once more, so he asked her to meet him at their favorite place. Sean had not spoken with her since *that day* when she decided against their elopement. Now he must tell her of *his* decision. It broke his heart to leave her and he knew it would break her heart, as well. He had agonized over this decision. How could he stay at home and not have the one he loved so dearly? And then, too, how could he not do his duty for America, the land that had given them so much?

Jessica was waiting in the clearing when he arrived. She ran to him and held him with a fierceness that took his breath away. "My darling, my darling," she cried. "I thought I would never hear from you. But you're here now and nothing else matters. I love you so, Sean!"

"I know, sweetheart, I know." He caressed her hair and kissed her moist lips.

"Oh, Sean, I've been crying for an eternity. I can't eat, can't sleep. I'm the unhappiest girl in the world. What can we do?"

He placed a finger under her chin and tilted her face upward to kiss her again. "Jessica, I have to tell you somethin'. I've made a decision. I can't bear our bein' apart. The torture of knowin' you are so near and yet . . ." His voice trailed off.

"What do you mean—a decision?" She looked searchingly into his eyes. The look of dejection on his face did not escape her. "I have a feeling that you're going to tell me something I will not like. What is it, Sean?"

He held her hands in his. Taking a long, deep and tremulous breath, he said, "Jessica, I love you with all my heart but the way things are—I can't stay here at home any longer. It's best I leave for awhile."

"Leave! What do you mean 'leave'?"

"Darlin', I've enlisted in the Army. Things are lookin' bad for Mr. Lincoln's government and I want to help. This land has been good to us."

Jessica exploded. "How could you, without even talking to me about it . . . you promised me you'd never leave me!" She broke down in tears.

"Jessica, please, I couldn't see any other way. When I come back maybe our parents . . . maybe they'll understand and give us their blessings."

"*When* you get back? Did you ever think, Sean, that you might be killed? Oh, God, I can't bear the thought. Why have you done this?" Her sobs grew louder.

"I'm torn between my love for you and what I believe is my duty. Under the circumstances, I feel there's no other way. Jessica, listen to me. This is for us. For our country. To keep the Union. After my service, I promise you, no matter what I have to do, we'll be together. I swear it!"

She stood there like the Biblical Lot's wife—turned to a pillar of stone. After a few moments, she patted her face dry and tried to smile. "Sean, I shall always love you. If you must go, then know that I'll be here waiting for you and praying that God watches over you. My heart goes with you. Be safe, my love, and come home to us."

They kissed passionately and, as dusk settled around them, emotions carried them to a new dimension. "I love you, Jessica. I need you and can't help wanting you so. I know we mustn't but I can't help it . . ."

"And I want you, Sean, forever. Love me, Sean. Love me *now*"

"Jessica, are you sure? I don't want you to be sorry—or hurt—"

"Shush, sweetheart, *now* so I may have a beautiful memory to cherish."

It was November and the air was cold but the young lovers, paying no heed to the chill, lay in a crude bed of fallen leaves and found fulfillment.

"Sean, now we are one before God." Jessica kissed him and snuggled closer, relishing the fleeting moments that would end all too soon.

*   *   *

On November 16, 1861, Sean said his goodbyes to his parents and a tearful Mrs. O. He shook hands with Reese, advising him to "take care of things until I get back". Eamon insisted on taking his son into the City to the recruitment station. Sean had packed a few personal items into a small hand case that he held on his lap as he sat beside his father. A silent Eamon steered the wagon toward Bloemendahl Road.

Sean broke the silence. "Da, I am truly sorry for the grief I'm causin' but this is somethin' I must do. It's terrible for me leavin' everyone I love but it's for somethin' I believe is important. Mr. Lincoln says we must preserve the Union and, Da, who's to do it if not the likes of us?"

"There's no arguin' with you now, son. 'Tis done. I only hope you will not pay too high a price for your hasty decision . . . and your patriotism. I pray the Lord will bring you back ta us."

Sean attempted to change the conversation. "I'm glad, Da, that you have Reese to help you. He'll be able to make the deliveries by himself because he's done it with me so often. The route is familiar to him."

A distracted Eamon mumbled, "Yes, yes, fer sure."

Poor Da. He looks like a beaten man. I've never seen him this way, Sean thought. He put his arms around his father. "I don't want to hurt you and Mam but I have to do this."

"Oh, Son, I'm afraid we have driven you to it and that is the worst of the matter. If anythin' should happen . . ." his voice faded.

Sean looked away from the tears in his father's eyes.

CHAPTER XV

*B*Y THE TIME *Lincoln was inaugurated on March 4, 1861,
South Carolina, Georgia, Louisiana, Mississippi, Florida,
Alabama and Texas had decided to secede from the Union. They voted
to form a new nation, adopting a constitution similar to that of the
United States. One difference, however, was the provision that the states
had the right to permit and regulate slavery. Jefferson Davis (a former
senator from Mississippi) was elected President of the Confederate states,
the assertion being that they represented a foreign power.*

*Lincoln strongly believed that the Constitution prohibited any state
from withdrawing from the Union. After the attack on Fort Sumter,
outraged Northerners demonstrated in the streets. Newspapers demanded
retaliation against the South, declaring that the defiance shown by the
seceded states, and the firing upon the Federal flag, made it an enemy of
the National government.*

*In April 1861, Lincoln called upon state militias of the Union "to
the aggregate number of seventy-five thousand . . . to maintain the
honor, integrity, and existence of our National Union". By December
1861, there were more than 640,000 volunteers, most of whom had
never experienced any military training. A good number of their officers
were volunteer businessmen, lawyers, politicians and even members of
the clergy, unlike those of the South who were graduates of West Point—
men born and bred in the tradition of the gentleman soldier.*

*Patriotism and a strong sense of adventure brought recruits in droves.
Most signed up for a 90-day term; many believed they would never see
action; many believed they would be home before the 90 days were up.
State capitals were brimming with regiments of volunteers awaiting*

orders to proceed to Washington. They were a colorful lot wearing whatever uniforms had been created for them in their respective cities—anything from Scotch kilts to the popular "Zouave" uniforms, copied from the French Algerians.

The colorful, unruly lot that descended upon Washington was welcomed with open arms. Business in houses of ill-repute and saloons boomed, as did the retail stores of every kind.

In July of 1861, 35,000 men of the Army of the Potomac faced their Confederate foes in the first major battle of the Civil War, at Bull Run (Manassas), and met with defeat. The 69th NYS Militia was mustered out after serving their term. The newly formed NYS Volunteers attached to Meagher's Brigade left New York for Washington, D. C., on November 18, 1861, where their duty was to defend the Capital.

Sean was one of the 745 men who left for Washington with the 69th New York Volunteers, in wagon trains and with antiquated weapons, the colors and regimental flags waving in the wind and their mounted officers in the lead. As they passed through village and town, they were greeted with cheers from people lining the streets and roadsides. They made camp by nightfall to eat some hot food around campfires and to rest. By dawn, they were on the move again to their destination—the outskirts of Alexandria, Virginia.

*　　*　　*

25 November 1861

Dear Mam and Da,

How are you? How are Mrs. O and Reese? Let me say I'm well and miss all of you. Please, do not worry, I'm with fine lads and courageous officers, some who fought in the Bull Run battle. Did you know about the flag ceremony on Madison Avenue in the City? Because the 69th was the first to reach its quota of men, they presented our regiment with the national Stars and Stripes and the regimental colors which were made by Tiffany & Company. Isn't that something! All us boys were so proud as we marched down the avenue. I'm sorry I couldn't tell you about it but you would have had the news too late, anyway.

Now here we are near Alexandria, Virginia, where we have set up camp—Camp California, they call it. We'll train here all winter. Not to worry, we are well fed and have proper, warm clothing. Mam and Da, even our souls are well taken care of. A French-Canadian Jesuit, Father Thomas Ouellet, keeps us in good spiritual health.

With deep affection for you all, I am, your son,

Sean

*   *   *

25 November 1861

Dear Reese,

How are you, old friend? I hope you are not too burdened with work, me not being there to help. It is a comfort to me knowing that you are there to help Mam and Da and Mrs. O'Rourke.

Do you ever get to see the Wahlberg's? Especially Jessica? I think of her all the time. I am enclosing a note for her which I hope you can leave under that big rock where I used to place messages. Please try to do this for me. She will be looking for my letters.

It's a rugged life in the Army, but I believe I am doing something important for this country, as the President says we are. Mr. Lincoln is a great man, to be honored and respected, and I do just that. I just hope and pray that we will be properly prepared for battle. Except for those who were at Bull Run, none of us knows how to shoot a rifle. However, I believe after training, we'll be fit and ready. All the boys are eager to do their bit.

I miss you, my friend, as I do my family. God bless you.

Sean

Everyday Jessica faithfully checked under the rock. Finally, early in December, she found Sean's letter. She could hardly contain herself as she opened it with trembling hands. Her breath caught in her throat as she read:

25 November 1861

Dearest Jessica, my love,

How I miss your sweet face and the smile that always dances around your precious mouth and puts a sparkle in your eye. And I miss the love we share. Every night, after we finish drilling and training and have our dinner, I just go to my bunk and think about you and all the plans I have for us when I come home. After lights-out, I fall asleep dreaming that you are beside me.

Be brave, my darling. Don't worry about me. I am fine and am with some courageous, wonderful men, who are just as homesick as I am but are here to do right for our country.

I'll have you back in my arms before you know it and we'll have a wonderful life together. My dearest Jessica, how I love you.

Forever yours,
Sean

As she read and reread the letter, tears fell uncontrolled. Finally, she threw herself down on the ground, sobbing so violently she felt her heart would burst. "Oh, Sean, Sean, my darling. Why? Why?" She calmed herself with the thought that at least now she could write to him.

Reese faithfully delivered all Sean's letters and Jessica devoted herself to writing to "her Sean" every day.

*   *   *

5 December 1861

Dear Mam and Da,

We are in training so much of the time that I cannot write as often as I would like. Marching and drilling, that's all we do, except for eating and other necessities. There are two other companies, the 88th New York and the 63rd New York that joined up to drill with us for the rest of the winter. We get along just fine as everybody is so friendly. Some of the boys play guitars and banjoes or fiddle a lively tune. That always cheers us up. Lots of evenings we sit around singing along or even just listening.

I was so happy to get your letter and package with the socks and Mrs. O's special biscuits. It's sure wonderful to have something from home. Please give Mrs. O a big hug for me.

Some of the boys here can't write too well so I've been helping them with their letters. The mother of one of the boys sent a handmade scarf for me. I was so grateful!

Say hello to Reese. God bless all of you.

Your loving son,

Sean

*   *   *

25 December 1861

Merry Christmas to you all!

I wish I was there to say it in person. Things here are good. We celebrated Christmas Eve in proper fashion. A fourteen year old boy who came to the war with his father, played the bagpipes as he played the violin. Some of us even danced Irish jigs and reels. We sat around the campfires singing songs that reminded us of home. And, yes, Mam, be happy to know that there was a midnight mass held at camp and most of us went. Father Ouellet takes good care of our souls.

My love to you all, your loving son,

Sean.

Christmas 1861, at the farm, was not a happy one. They all felt the absence of Sean at the dinner table. When they said grace, they added a prayer for his safety and well-being. His letters brought them consolation but Maureen could never control the emotion that welled up from deep within.

With the war escalating, greater demands for crops in the North brought about a tremendous increase in productivity; the *American Agriculturist* urged farmers to do so with the slogan, "One bushel more". Northern farmers cooperated and reaped the benefits.

Maureen now worked the farm alongside Eamon and Reese. Mrs. O was in charge of the kitchen and office. Things went smoothly for them. But the void left by Sean was an ever-present ache. Reese usually went into town on errands, but, once in a while, Maureen and Eamon would drive the wagon in for sundry supplies or personal items. On one such occasion, while they were in the general store where Maureen was selecting some fabric, a familiar voice called to them.

"Maureen, Eamon, how nice to see you. It's been a long time." Betty Wahlberg embraced Maureen.

"Oh, Betty, sure 'tis nice ta see you. How is Morris and your daughter?" In spite of the brouhaha over the young ones, Maureen could not be less than civil to someone who was a friend.

"Morris is just fine." She hesitated. "But my Jessica is not. I imagine you have the same problem with Sean, no? I hear he is not home, that he has gone to fight for our country. Such a fine, brave boy. You must be proud."

"Yes, Betty, my Sean is in the Army. I only hope the good Lord will bring him back ta me. My regards ta your own." She turned to Eamon, who said nothing. "Come, Eamon, we must be gettin' on. 'Tis late and there's work ta be done."

Eamon tipped his hat to Betty. "I hope we can have tea together soon. Give my best ta Morris. Good day."

When they climbed back into their wagon, Maureen turned to Eamon, anger flashing in her eyes. "Now why in God's name did you say that? 'Tis their daughter's fault our son ran off ta the Army!"

"Oh, Maureen, do not say that. Yes, the boy loves the girl and sad he was not ta court her, but you must admit, he was all fired up by Mr. Lincoln's call ta arms. He believes he is goin' ta fight fer a good cause."

"A better cause would have been ta stay here with his family where he is needed."

Eamon put his arms around his wife. He knew the anguish she was feeling only too well. "Darlin', the Lord will protect him fer he is a good lad. Sean will be home with us before you can dance a jig. So come now, luv, wipe the tears from your lovely eyes and we shall go home fer the nice dinner Mrs. O is preparin'. Sean will be jist foine, I promise you."

"Oh, sweet Jesus!" was all Maureen could say.

CHAPTER XVI

*P*RESIDENT LINCOLN'S CALL *for 75,000 men to defend the Capital brought more than double that amount of volunteer militiamen. With the raising of this tremendous army came the need for increased production of uniforms, boots, wagons, saddlery, harness equipment, rifles and artillery. Jobs were plentiful. Immigrants flocked into New York and Boston in droves. However, the labor force was not enough to meet the high demands of production. Although the Singer sewing machine was invented in 1851, never had it enjoyed the importance now thrust upon it because of the need for Union army uniforms. So, too, the need for boots made acceptance of Lyman Blake's shoe stitching machine easy. In short, manufacturing of products and substitutes therefor became highly profitable. The railroads and steamboats were packed full with supplies and raw materials and the products made from them.*

* * *

Near the end of February 1862, after the New York State Volunteers had served their ninety days, Brigadier General Thos. Francis Meagher, who officially took command on February 5, 1862, announced, "Anyone who reenlists will be granted a week's leave to go home, after which time the regiment will be awaiting orders of deployment. Those who do not reenlist will be required to stay until orders are received to muster them out."

After a rousing speech by their Commander, the men cheered. Most of them lined up to reenlist, shouting patriotic slogans and shaking each other's hands. Sean was one of them: young men, their innocence as yet untainted by battle; older men, eager to add meaning to their lives; all of them, inspired by the same fire of patriotism.

Sean wrote several letters home but said nothing about the possibility of a furlough. He wanted it to be a surprise. All he could think about was reuniting with the folks and seeing Jessica again. Telling his parents about his reenlistment would be difficult; telling Jessica would be no easier.

While at Camp California, Sean received mail from his parents about conditions on the farm:

Dear Sean,

How are you, dear son? All of us here miss you and pray for your safety and good health. We are getting to be real dandies. We have hired a young girl for $1.25 a day, plus room and board, to help your mother with her house work.

Would you believe, Mrs. O's office has now become our 'library' as we are obtaining books to better ourselves in reading and writing. We even bought some heavy bookshelves and a grand gentleman's chair for me to sit and have a smoke of an evening, that is of course when Mrs. O is done with her bookkeeping. Your mother and I and sometimes Mrs. O and Reese sit at the writing table and study our books. Other times, we play 'Yankee Trader' or cribbage. Whenever we go into town we get a copy of Harper's Monthly. We have been reading the reports of the battlefields by John De Forest. It frightens your mother but she enjoys the advertisements, recipes and patterns in the magazine. We are hoping to get a book or two by Dickens or Cooper. Do you have any books to read in Camp? Do you have time to read, I should say. We are looking forward to your next letter.

The good Lord be with you, Sean.

Your loving father and mother, with regards from Mrs. O and Reese

In another letter, Eamon wrote, "Soon we hope to purchase a horse-powered mower and rake which will be a big help cultivating and planting. Mam says she will learn how to work the machine so she can help with the crops, now that she has a 'girl' to do the domestic work. She is something! Full of spunk!"

The highlight of the letter was a description of the new "privies" in the backyard: "the door to the ladies' side is marked with a crescent moon; the men's, with a sun". Sean read this part aloud to his comrades and they all had a good laugh.

The improvement shown in his father's writing impressed Sean. He was happy that spending all that time "at the writing table" paid off.

A steady stream of letters came from Jessica, all of which spoke of her love, her longing, and her ever-constant concern for his safety. Alone in his tent, just before dark every evening, he would read and reread her words. His heart ached for her. He relived those beautiful intimate moments in their trysting place in the woods: the warmth of her supple body, the cries of passion, the sweet caress of her soft, moist lips—how she had whispered, "I love you with all my heart, Sean, forever and ever". Every night, he prayed that he may return to her and spend the rest of his life blessed with that love.

*   *   *

The 69th had marched and ridden in wagons down to Washington. Now they would be returning to New York by way of the Washington and Old Dominion Railroad to Leesburg and, the rest of the way, on adjunct railroads which would eventually bring them to downtown New York City. Sean could hardly wait. The faster, the better.

In his last letter to Reese, he instructed him to be at the Center Street Railroad Terminal on March 4th, at about 3 p.m. "If we are not on time, finish your deliveries to the greengrocers and then return to the station. I'll wait where the horse-and-wagons are allowed to park. Be careful, friend, the City will be crowded with servicemen and their families. A recently arrived New York volunteer told me it is hectic there these days. Oh, yes, watch out for the Broadway Squad—they are always out in full force to manage horse-drawn traffic. If you are stopped for any reason, be sure to tell them that you are waiting for Pvt. Sean McCullough of the 69th Irish Brigade. That'll endear you to any Irish policeman."

Sean further advised Reese that if his company did not arrive as planned, he was to wait no longer than 7 p.m. and return home. Sean did not want his folks worrying. "I'll find my way, if I have to. One of those horse-cars will bring me close enough to home."

Center Street was a frenzy of activity. Police whistles could be heard above the din of people's voices, horses' hoofs and carriage wheels. The men of the 69th did not arrive until 6 p.m. Men, women and children swarmed around them, asking questions about the war and next of kin. Sean moved past the clusters of people, hoping to locate Reese. It grew close to 7 o'clock and the sea of humanity surrounding him seemed unending. The pack on his back slowed him up a bit. As he made his way, he was grateful that he left some personal equipment and heavy winter wear at the Camp.

Suddenly, he heard a familiar voice. "Sean, Sean, here. I'm over here. Look to your left." Sure enough, there was Reese with a big smile on his face, holding the reins of their old horse, that Sean had named Excalibur. Jumping off the wagon, Reese threw his arms around Sean. "Sure am glad to see you. Things are so crazy hereabouts, I was scared I wouldn't find you. As it is, I looked twice at you in them baggy red trousers and bright blue jacket before I realized it was you. What kinda hat is that, anyhow?"

"They call it a fez. This uniform is copied after the Zouave outfits that the French Algerians wore. You think this is funny? You should see what the 79th New York was wearing when they got to Washington. Scottish kilts, no less! I tell you, we may not be the best trained army but we sure are the most colorful!" Sean placed his hand on Reese's shoulder. "Good to see you, my friend.

Now let's get away from all these shenanigans and head for home."
Sean patted Excalibur's nose and whispered in his ear; the horse
responded with a spirited whinny.

Back on the farm, Maureen was concerned because Reese had
not yet returned. "It is 8 o'clock already. Where can the boy be?
When he goes to the City alone, it troubles me. Why did you not
go with him, Eamon?"

"Oh, luv, you are upset for no reason. Is it the first time now
that he has gone alone? No, it is not, so stop frettin' and come here
and give us a kiss."

"Och, Eamon McCullough, do not make a fool of me. You
will not get a kiss until I see Reese and the wagon return." She
went to the front window, parted the curtains and peered into the
dark. "Oh, thank the Lord, I see him comin' up the path. Eamon,
come quick, I think there is someone sittin' beside him."

As the wagon grew nearer, Eamon could not believe his eyes.
He flung open the front door and rushed out.

"Hello, Da."

Eamon shouted, "Oh, Lord, is it really you, son? Maureen
come quick, it is our own dear boy come back to us." He embraced
his son. Tears filled his eyes.

Maureen came running, followed by Mrs. O. "Oh, sweet
Jaysus, is it really my Sean? My boy, oh, my boy, it is you indeed.
My prayers have been answered." She held onto Sean, kissing his
face again and again, as she murmured thanks.

"How about a big hug for me, laddie-boy?" Mrs. O gently
pushed Maureen aside and wrapped Sean in one of her famous
bear hugs.

"Why did you not tell us you were comin' home, son, so we
could have a proper welcome ready? And you, Reese, knowin' all
along and not sayin' a word!" Maureen complained.

"Now, Mam," Sean cajoled, hugging her, "you wouldn't have
Reese spoil my surprise? Come, put a smile on your lovely face . . ."

"And give me my kiss," Eamon demanded.

Maureen did as they asked.

Once inside the house, Sean asked to be excused so that he could get out of his "Zouaves" and back into his own clothes. How wonderful to be home! The last three months were unreal—like a bad dream. The farm seemed so peaceful and yet he knew the war must be taking its toll. He looked about his room. Nothing had been altered. His books, his desk . . . everything just as he had left it. Many a night he wished he was back but then he would think about why he left in the first place. It was the least he could do for the country that had provided such opportunity. Although, Sean wondered, would he have enlisted so impetuously, had it not been for the controversy over Jessica. Jessica! I must see her tomorrow. I hope she found the message Reese left for her. With these thoughts racing through his mind, he rejoined the family in the sitting room.

They all asked questions at once about his experiences. Sean described the long hours of skirmishing drills and battalion drills. "But, weather conditions are the worst of it. We had the hardest storm of the season back in January. When that wind blows around the tents and sleet starts pelting the roofs, it sounds like gunshots; but, when the rain freezes as it falls and forms a coat over the tents, that and the little camp stoves warm us up a bit. Pity the poor boys on guard duty, standin' out in that weather for hours."

Between sniffles and moaning sounds, Maureen asked, "Do you get enough to eat? Do you have warm clothes? Are you gettin' our letters?"

"Yes, to all your questions, Mam. I am so glad you and Da are improvin' so much in your readin' and writin'."

Sean decided he would say nothing of his reenlistment until it was time to leave. Right now, they believed he would be returning home for good within a short time.

Eamon asked, "Did you not fulfill your volunteer time with the 69th? It was 90 days, was it not? Why do you have to go back?"

"Just some red tape. Official papers have to come to our commander before he can muster us out." Sean quickly changed the subject. "Are you gettin' the allotment drafts I signed for? Most of us are sendin' money home. It keeps us from squanderin' our pay at the sutlers or grog shops."

Eamon nodded. 'Yes, son, we are receivin' the money and it is all bein' set aside for you in that new bank that opened up here."

"Thank you, Da. I appreciate that." He continued. "You should see all the gear we are obliged to carry . . . weighs about fifty pounds. The best bit of equipment, though, is a 'housewife' for each of us . . ."

"What?" Maureen cried. "What do you mean, a housewife? Sean . . . !"

Sean laughed then explained. "Mam. a housewife is a sewing kit. A very handy item to have, under the circumstances."

Maureen blushed at her rash outburst, saying quietly, "Yes, I am sure it is."

Sean went on, in a more serious vein, "But, there are lots of complaints about some of the other equipment. Things are fallin' apart. It seems that some of the government contractors are usin' shoddy materials."

"What a disgrace!" Eamon was furious. "Makin' inferior things for our boys. They should put them all in jail."

Sean decided he wouldn't mention the antiquated rifled muskets and small arms.

The rest of the evening was spent in talk of the farm and how business was progressing. The hired girl helped Maureen prepare a late repast and, after cleaning up, retired to her upstairs room. Before long, Maureen suggested, "Well, I think it is time you got some rest, Sean. You look a little worn."

"Yes, Mam, I am a bit weary—the long trip and all."

"See you bright and early in the mornin', son." Eamon took his hand in his.

"Yes, Da," Sean hugged his parents. "I'm so happy to be home—even for a little while.

Maureen's eyes widened. Eamon squeezed her hand. She said nothing.

CHAPTER XVII

MORNING COULD NOT come fast enough for Sean. He would have to give his parents some excuse for taking the wagon. He hoped Jessica would be waiting for him, as planned. Luck was on his side. As he entered the kitchen, he heard his mother telling Reese to go into the village to pick up supplies.

"I'll take a ride with you," Sean offered.

"Not until you have a good breakfast under your belt," Maureen said.

Sean and Reese exchanged glances of relief. He ate as quickly as he could without drawing his mother's notice then kissed her on the forehead. "See you later, Mam."

Maureen smiled as she watched them ride away. The good Lord had delivered.

Jessica was already waiting when the wagon pulled into the clearing. Sean remarked, "Reese, how lovely she looks, my beautiful girl."

Jessica was dressed in a simple, long gingham-checkered dress, the bodice of which pinched in at her slender waist and accentuated her full bosom. Her bonnet tied under her chin with wide ribbons and was trimmed with a ruffle and a cluster of flowers at the side. The long blonde hair Sean loved to touch cascaded from beneath the brim and framed her delicate features.

Reese brought the wagon to a stop and waved to Jessica. He told Sean, "Be back for you in two hours," as Sean jumped down and ran to embrace his love. He lifted her high off the ground and swung her around until she begged him to stop.

"Sean, please, I can hardly catch my breath." Her laughter between gasps sounded like the tinkling of piano keys.

Sean could not contain his emotions. "Oh, my darlin', my own sweet love, my life . . ." When he finally put her down, she flung her arms around him.

"I shall never let go of you, Sean McCullough. My life is empty without you. I do dearly love you so."

"And I, you. You have my heart. How I longed to hold you close these many months and now, at last, here you are in my arms." He lifted her again, holding her tightly, carrying her to the niche in the woods where they had first surrendered to their desire. "'Tis a consummation devoutly to be wished'," Sean whispered.

Jessica giggled. "Shakespeare wrote it but it sounds better coming from your lips."

He kissed her passionately and laid her down gently onto a bed of fallen leaves, after he spread out the soft blanket she always carried with her when she came there to write. The trees surrounding them were barren but the branches diffused the light of sun and sky, enveloping the young lovers in soft shadows.

Sean hungrily kissed her face, her lips, the soft hollow of her neck. She, in turn, played her fingers over his body, gently caressing him. Overwhelmed by their longing, they yielded to the moment.

"Oh, my love, my dearest one, how I wanted you . . ." she was in tears.

He kissed her eyelids and the tip of her nose. "I'm here. I'm here. I shall always be with you."

They lay quietly for awhile, holding each other. Jessica said, "Promise me, Sean, that you will never leave me again. I can't live without you. You aren't going back, are you, Sean? I shall die if you do."

He placed his fingers over her mouth. She was getting hysterical and he couldn't bear to see her anguish. Dreading to tell her the truth, but knowing that he must, he took both her hands in his, saying, "Jessica, listen to me. I don't want to hurt you but I can't lie to you. I love you more than my life . . ."

She stopped him. "Oh, Sean, I've got a terrible feeling about what you are going to say." She began to cry again.

"Sweet one, listen to me. Reese will be back soon and I don't want to leave you this way. Try to understand. I love you but I love our country, too, and I am proud to serve in this time of unrest. Darlin', I have reenlisted. Please don't cry, Jessica. Please try to understand. It'll all be over soon, my love, and I'll be home for good."

"But, Sean, if you have to go into battle you could be hurt, or even killed! Oh, my God, I can't bear it!" Her body trembled.

"I promise you, Jessica, I *will* come back and we'll spend the rest of our lives together, with or without the blessings of our parents. That I promise you faithfully." He held her in his arms until Reese appeared. He told her, "I'll be over tomorrow to say 'hello' to your parents. I do believe that is the right thing to do. Our families have always been friendly. Now, let me see a smile on your pretty face. Everything will be just fine."

"Sean, I hope and pray you are right."

"Don't say a word about my visit. I'll just show up. A surprise!" He hopped into the wagon and threw her a kiss. Reese bid her a "good day".

The next morning at 6 a.m., Sean arose to help Reese and his father milk the cows, feed the plow horse and chickens, and lay fresh straw on the floor of the barn. After a hearty breakfast of steak, eggs and Mrs. O's apple pie, Sean announced, "Mam, Da, I would like to take the wagon. I am going to visit the Wahlberg's . . ."

Maureen's strident voice cut him off. "Sean, you will do no such thing! It can only cause trouble for us all."

"Trouble?" How can it cause trouble? Our families got along so nicely until I told you Jessica and I are in love . . ."

Eamon cut in. "Now, Sean, your mother is only thinkin' of

what is best for you. We have discussed this before and you know the position of the Church . . ."

"Damn the position of the Church! Damn the salvation of my soul! I love Jessica and I don't care that she is not Catholic. I want to spend my life here on earth with her. Heaven can wait!"

Maureen was horrified. "Oh, Lord. Oh, Sweet Jesus. What have I done to be punished this way? My own son, a blasphemer!"

Eamon decided on the path of least resistance. "Now, wife, the boy only wants to pay his respects to the girl and her parents. What harm can there be in that?" He knew the position of the Wahlberg's was as firm as theirs. His son's visit was purely a social amenity. He looked meaningfully at Sean who immediately modified his tone.

"Mam, I just think it is right that I present myself to the Wahlberg's. Not to worry, I'm not going to run away with their daughter. But, in truth, I do want to see her. Mam, it won't be long before I return to the 69th. Can I at least enjoy my time here now?"

The mention of his leaving brought on more of Maureen's wailing.

Eamon put his arms around her. "Now, luv, let the boy do as he wishes. He has little time here as it is."

She turned away. Eamon winked at Sean. "Be back by sundown, son."

Betty could barely contain her composure when she opened the door and saw Sean. She was fond of the boy—always had been. She put her arm in his and ushered him into the front parlor. "Sean, my dear, it is so wonderful to see you looking so well." She meant every word even though she inwardly feared what his presence could mean. "Jessica," she called upstairs, "look who's here."

Feigning surprise, Jessica welcomed Sean. "I am so happy to see you." She resisted the temptation to hug him, to hold him close.

"Darling, go get your father," Betty said. "He's out back with the hired man getting some produce ready for market."

They spent a lovely afternoon. Betty served tea and some of her fine baking as they sat and chatted. The intensity of feeling every time Jessica and Sean looked at each other was not lost on the Wahlberg's.

Morris asked, "How long are you here for, Sean?"

Sean explained his furlough and his reenlistment. Jessica held back tears. Her parents were torn between a feeling of relief and a deep concern for Sean. No matter what, they did not wish any harm to befall him. Nothing was said for several moments, all dealing with their innermost thoughts. Breaking the silence, Betty asked, "Sean, will you have supper with us? You're welcome."

"No, thank you, Mrs. Wahlberg. I promised to be home by sundown. If you don't mind, I would like to come visit again before I return to camp."

"Of course, darling," Betty warmly replied.

All that Jessica could think about was the next day—in the woods.

The balance of Sean's furlough was spent in visits and clandestine meetings with Jessica. He helped with chores as much as possible and was relieved when Eamon told him that he had hired help, whenever necessary, while Sean was away. "And do not forget, we have Reese. He is a fine lad and my right hand. It will all do until you come back."

Sean admired his father. He decided that on his next time at home, he would settle the matter about wanting to marry Jessica, sure that his father would come 'round and bring Mam with him—and that the Wahlberg's would do likewise. But, at any cost, he will be with his Jessica, he vowed.

CHAPTER XVIII

*T*HE 69*TH* NEW York of the Irish Brigade earned a reputation for hard and courageous fighting. The question, "Where are my green flags?" was common among commanding officers who looked for the support of the brave men who fought under those colors.

In 1862, when the Union Army was reorganized into corps and divisions, the Irish Brigade was part of the II Corps and designated as the Second Brigade of the First Division, under General Israel B. Richardson. The other companies in the Division were the 63*rd* N. Y. and the 28*th* Mass., the 88*th* N. Y. and 116*th* Penn. That year, the 69*th* fought in many skirmishes, displaying a valor admired by their officers and generals: the Peninsular Campaign, Battle of Fair Oaks Station, Battle of Gaines Mill, Battle of Savage Station, Malvern Hill Battle. Then, on 17 September, the Irish Brigade faced the Confederate Colonel Posey and his Mississippi Brigade at the Battle of Antietam in Sharpsburg, Maryland. The plan had been to overrun the Confederate position, holding their fire until they were in the face of the rebels. They took tremendous losses as Posey's men fired volley after volley as they approached. The Brigade then halted to send "buck and ball" into the ranks of the Mississippians. Exposed and on high ground, the Brigade continued to suffer casualties. Gen. Meagher attempted several bayonet charges. These men were immediately shot down by the hard fighting 4*th* and 30*th* North Carolina regiments. What was left of the Brigade was finally relieved by the arrival of Gen. Caldwell's brigade.

On 12 December, the Irish Brigade faced another disaster. Gen. Meagher ordered his men to take Marye's Heights in the town of Fredericksburg. They fought fearlessly to take that stone wall. Many

*died as they marched uphill, climbing over a wooden post fence in the
process, 50 yards from the wall. Confederate rifles and muskets opened
fire as the Brigade stood its ground until the order to lie down and
shoot. Only the right flank skirmishers were left unscathed. Finally, on
the 15th of December a truce was called so that the wounded could be
recovered. Unfortunately, many had succumbed to their injuries and
harsh weather.*

*   *   *

Sean was one of the lucky ones in the Battle of Fredericksburg.
He was in the right flank of skirmishers, the only ones who suffered
no casualties. The New York Tribune and the New York Herald
carried details of the severity of the battle. When the McCullough's
read of the enormous numbers of dead and wounded, Maureen
was close to collapse. A distraught Eamon tried to comfort her.
"Come now, wife, we have received no word that our son is a
casualty. Let us keep hope in our hearts and pray to the Lord that
he is safe."

Endless weeks went by filled with dread and anxiety. Finally!
A letter from Sean. Eamon read it aloud:

23 December 1862

Dear Mam and Da,

 I am happy to say that I am alive and well, except for a
few nicks and scratches. You probably read about the fierce
battle at Fredericksburg, Virginia (December 12 to 15) in
which our Brigade took part. General Meagher's sons of
Erin fought so bravely that General Pickett's rebs cheered us
right there on the battlefield. If we had had more men, we
could have taken that position and routed the gray backs.

 As usual, there were reporters and photographers on a
nearby hill. Did the papers carry the details and pictures of
the battle? Did you see them? To say the truth, I hope you
did not because you could only suffer distress from it. I am
truly sorry I could not write any earlier but we marched here

to Falmouth, Virginia, to set up winter quarters where we are bivouacked, waiting for new recruits.

My dear family, I miss you all and love you dearly. I pray God watch over you and protect all of us in this noble cause. May we soon enjoy peace in this land we hold so dear. Please remember me to Mrs. O and Reese. I wish you all a blessed Christmas. May the new year bring an end to this terrible struggle and find our country united in peace.

Your loving son, Sean

Tearfully, Maureen took the letter out of Eamon's hands and pressed it first to her lips and then to her bosom. "Oh, Eamon, it is the finest gift that the Lord has provided us."

Mrs. O sniffled and wiped away a tear. Reese remained silently thankful.

Jessica, too, received a long awaited letter from Sean:

23 December 1862, Falmouth, Virginia

My Darling,

By the grace of God, I have survived some of the bloodiest conflicts of this uncivil war. I am sure you have been following the newspaper accounts and I truly regret any grief it may have caused you. But, I am here in Falmouth, Virginia, and am fine.

Every spare moment is spent thinking of you—how sweet and warm your lips taste. Memories fill my body and soul with longing. Reliving the precious moments of our togetherness fires my determination to stay alive, to come home to you, my precious one.

I love you with all my heart.

Yours forever, Sean

Tears flowed profusely as she read the words of her beloved. "Oh, dear God, please bring him back to me," she prayed aloud.

*   *   *

Winter grew long and hard and bitter cold. In February of 1863, Mrs. O complained of back pain and harbored a suspicious cough. In spite of medical attention, she developed pneumonia. Maureen sat by her side every day, fearful of the growing complications. She made sure the fireplace was well lit all the time and that the bedding was clean and comfortable. Mrs. O said, "Oh, darlin', ya need not fuss so. I am an old lady and 'tis time ta see my maker."

"Mrs. O," Maureen would chide, "please do not speak so. You are not goin' to see anyone. You are stayin' here with us." Inwardly, she was apprehensive—it was impossible to think of life without her. Yet, Mrs. O grew weaker and weaker. Her condition worsened. One day, she told Maureen, "Dear, get me that little velvet box out of the top drawer of the dresser." She gently removed from it a true jet carved brooch. Taking Maureen's hand in hers, she said, "I wore this after my mother passed on. I want you to wear it after—for me."

Maureen began to sob as Mrs. O pressed the pin into her hand and spoke her last words: "the Lord save our Sean." She slowly closed her eyes as Maureen leaned over to kiss her cheek.

The family had set aside a corner of the farm as a burial place. Now it would receive its first occupant. Eamon prepared a tombstone that depicted two angels, with the inscription, "In the arms of Jesus", beneath which he carved an empty rocking chair, in sentimental memory of the dearly departed woman they all loved so much. Maureen saved a lock of Mrs. O's hair to encase under crystal in a locket which she now wore. She nervously fingered the brooch pinned to her jacket as Eamon read a prayer and said some appropriate words. The Wahlberg's stood nearby to pay their last respects.

"I have lost my best friend," Maureen whispered as she placed a bouquet of flowers on the grave.

Reese murmured softly, "She has gone home."

*   *   *

Sean remained at Falmouth, Virginia, until April of 1863. He wrote several letters home. When he received the news of Mrs. O's death, he was devastated and spoke of his regret that he was not there to lend support to the family. When he read of Mrs. O's dying words for his safety, he broke down. "Oh, to have been there to hold her hand one last time!" he sobbed.

*   *   *

On the 1ˢᵗ of July 1863, almost 200,000 men on horseback, on foot, with moving artillery, stretched across wide fields in Pennsylvania, in a town called Gettysburg—and the Irish regiment was there. After a campaign of many months, a small contingent of Confederates had penetrated the area and an exchange of fire with Union soldiers triggered one of the most important battles of the War Between the States.

Sean, now a sergeant, stood with his company (one of seven infantry corps) as they listened to General George G. Meade issue orders. Their green flag, next to Old Glory, fluttered in the breeze together with the regimental colors of the Second Army Corps of the Union Army. Detailing their strategy, the Commander reminded them, "Remember, boys, do not let the Rebs capture our flags. Those flags must never fall into their hands to become trophies. If you see a flag bearer in mortal danger, raise that flag. It must not fall."

Shouts of "Never!" echoed through the ranks.

On that first day, outnumbered Union forces suffered huge losses. Wave upon wave of men advanced and fell on both sides. Sean knew this was their fiercest battle yet. Long lines of troops faced each other, taking on deadly gunfire and bayonet charges as bullets and balls rained upon both sides. When Sean saw the bearer of their green flag going down, he rushed to his side and hoisted the flag above his head. It was not long before the Confederates overran their position. Sean was quick to wrap the flag around his body, under his jacket. "I will die with it, if I must," he shouted to his men. "This is a bad day for the Irish and the other lads." He gave the order to regroup for the next charge.

The air was filled with smoke and the stench of battle. They could hear the cries of the wounded and the dying. They could hear their commander yelling, "Where are my reinforcements? What is happening . . . ?" Futile questions rent the air. The carnage continued until both sides agreed to retreat to tend to their wounded and rest before the next engagement. Unfortunately, that first day, the Confederates took many prisoners. Sean was among the captured.

On July 3, 1863, the tide turned at Gettysburg and the Union forces wrested the victory from the Confederate Army. However, of their 82,289 engaged forces, 23,049 were casualties. The Confederates, under General Robert E. Lee, numbered 75,000, of which 28,049 were either wounded, killed, or missing. The bloody horror of lives sacrificed there prompted Lincoln's government to issue a proclamation of the draft which resulted in rioting in New York City, at which time more than a dozen New York regiments, veterans of Gettysburg, returned to help restore order.

Maureen and Eamon stopped sending Reese into the City to make deliveries because of the unrest that preceded the riots. At first, the demonstrations were against the Federal conscription of Lincoln's administration but they soon deteriorated into bloody race riots, reflecting the smoldering resentment and fear of Negroes coming North and working for less pay. The McCullough's worried that Reese would be in harm's way.

When Eamon went into the City, he was eyewitness to the violence they had heard about. Learning that some of the New York regiments were there, they prayed they would hear from Sean. His last letter, dated 28 June 1863, told them of the long and tiresome marches and his arrival in Gettysburg. "There are no Confederate forces here, Mam and Da," he had written, "so please do not worry." By the time his letter was received, news of the Battle of Gettysburg and the Union victory made headlines. Everyone dreaded the inevitable lists of wounded, missing, and dead.

Soon the McCullough's found Sean's name listed among the wounded taken prisoner. The relief of knowing he was alive was shattered by the fear of what it could mean to be a captive of the South.

CHAPTER XIX

B ELLE ISLE PRISON was just above the city of Richmond, Va., on the rapids of the James River and connected to the mainland by two railroad bridges and a wagon bridge. No more than a mile long and half-a-mile wide, it was built to hold a few thousand inmates, at most. The numbers there had now swelled to ten thousand. The area, nothing more than an enclosure built around rows of tents, was the unhappy place to which Sean and some of his men were taken after that first bloody day at Gettysburg. Sean anguished over his inability to "stay in the fight" but kept encouraging his men. "Do not worry, boys. Our Union forces will soon liberate us."

Sean wrote to his parents as often as he could; he also wrote to Jessica. He rarely told of the horrors that confronted him in battle but now in Belle Isle, he found it difficult to refrain from describing his unbearable existence.

15 August 1863

Dear Jessica,

My darling, I hope you are well and that you long for me as I do you.

I am a prisoner here in Belle Isle, Va., in a camp in which human beings are forced to live under the most despicable conditions. The sick and wounded are all about us, lying unattended for the most part. The smell of death is everywhere. I thank God that I was taken with barely a

scratch and pray I will soon be exchanged and allowed to go
back to my company.

Every day one hundred soldiers march across the bridge
to this island to serve as guards. You never saw a more corrupt
bunch. They traffic in smuggled or stolen items which they
sell to us, deprived as we are! Even the "hospital nurses",
men who merely pretend to care for the sick and wounded
take things, including our government food rations, and sell
them out on the street.

We just sit around in our tents or walk about as much
as we are permitted. Outside, we look longingly at the little
bridge, not too far off. It is called the "bridge of sighs".
Several men tried to swim across the swirling waters and
drowned. Looking at the treacherous current, it is easy to
understand why.

I miss you so, dear heart, and I look forward to holding
you in my arms, loving you, breathing in the sweet scent of
your body. Only the thought of being together gives me the
courage to go on and the hope to endure in this uncivil war.
You are my precious girl.

May the Lord bless our cause. Long may the Stars and
Stripes wave in freedom.

My warmest regards to your mother and father. I wish
them well.

I love you with all my heart.

                                    Your Sean

As time passed, Sean bolstered the morale of his men whenever
he heard expressions of defeat. "Now, men, we have marched in
the burning heat of summer, through the biting cold of winter
and fought well in the roar and fury of battle. As a tribute to those
brave men who fell, we must remain strong to fight another day
for the country we love, and with fearless hearts, to defend our flag
to the death." His eloquence inspired his men and gave them
renewed hope.

When he wrote to his parents, he spoke little of his awful plight but instead only of his "wish to return soon to the field" and his anticipation of "an early, glorious determination of victory for the Union".

*   *   *

The prisoners of Belle Isle spent a brutal summer and winter, alternating between excessive heat and freezing cold. The expected early releases of prisoners never materialized. Many suffered. Many died. Finally, at the end of February 1864, after seven months of captivity, Sean and some of the other prisoners were informed that they were being moved to Camp Sumter—Andersonville—Georgia. Actually the move was for security reasons but the prisoners were assured they would receive better rations at Andersonville while awaiting exchange.

Andersonville Prison was established near the town of Americus, on 24 February 1864, primarily as a temporary holding area for prisoner exchange. The exchange system failed when the Federal government stopped the previously agreed to program. The decision was attributed, in part, to the refusal of the Confederacy to exchange Union officers for black soldiers.

The prison was nothing more than a stockade with "pigeon roosts"— sentry boxes—at intervals of 30 yards. A stream flowing through the prison yard supplied most of the water. A "deadline" was established nineteen feet from the wall which prisoners were forbidden to cross, under penalty of death.

In a compound meant to house no more than 13,000 men, the population quickly accelerated to 20,000 by June 1864, and, shortly thereafter, to more than 33,000. With 400 men arriving daily, together with the exchange breakdown, the Confederate government was unable to provide adequate housing, food, clothing and medical care. Conditions were deplorable. All suffered immeasurably. Almost 13,000 died.

*   *   *

Life in Andersonville taxed even the strongest of mind and body. Sean never felt so helpless in all his young life.

30 March 1864

Dear Mam and Da,

I am writing to tell you, luckily, I am well and have been here in Andersonville Prison for a few weeks. Did you receive my mail from Belle Isle? I hope so. I am sorely lacking decent clothing and wholesome food. What we wouldn't give for fresh fruit or a decent potato for the poor lads down with scurvy!

There is always talk of us being exchanged and we pray it is so. Some of the guards try to be encouraging. That helps keep spirits up and even the will to live. Without hope I think many prisoners would give in to despair and die.

Dear loved ones, if I were an artist I would paint a picture of this place, with all its horrors, so that our leaders in Washington could see the inhumanity that thousands of Union soldiers are suffering. I do not like to write of such things but the disease, the poor sanitation, and malnutrition are outrageous. I must speak out. Da, do you think your friends at Tammany could put some pressure on the government? Something must be done about this hell on earth.

With deep love for you both, I remain
Your devoted son, Sean.

*   *   *

15 June 1864

Dear Mam and Da,

I have endured this hell, by the grace of the Almighty, barely surviving a terrible winter and now, the beginning of a suffocating summer. Many are sick with fever and many die every day—the despair of it all killing them as sure as the fever. I believe I could not have fought off the disease if it were not for a Lt. Abrams, a Yankee officer of the Jewish faith who gave me a blanket when I had the awful chilblains. He was also kind enough to supply me with medication, fresh fruit and potatoes which he bought from the guards, who are always anxious to get their hands on Union greenbacks. Lt. Abrams and I enjoy some wonderful conversations and he is indeed a fine friend. I told him I did not realize that there were Jews in the Union Army. "There are thousands," he said, "who are happy to fight with their Christian comrades for one cause, one country, and the Union."

He told me an interesting little story about the town of Manassas. It is actually named after a Jew who ran a small lodging house in the mountain passes where travelers would make an overnight stop on their way to Richmond. It became quite a famous place in the days of the stage coaches. Anyone inquiring about somewhere to stay halfway on their journey was told, "Stop at Manasseh's". The place retained the name, although it is now spelled differently. The first and second battles of Bull Run were fought there.

My dear parents, conditions here are unbelievable. Our own men take advantage of us. Those who have enough money get things like bread and pies or whiskey and plugs of tobacco. They bribe the guards and set up shop at night to sell these things to our own boys, at a large profit. Can you imagine that? I guess desperate times create desperate measures, but I find it hard to accept such disregard for comrades who are already suffering beyond endurance.

I pray you are both find and that you are able to manage the farm with Reese's help. I close with the wish that the good Lord will deliver us from this peril and that the Union will be victorious.

Your loving son, Sean

*   *   *

The McCullough's spent most of their waking hours worrying about their son. Soon, they were faced with another concern. Hearing that the government was now taking Negro troops to serve in the Union Army, Reese spoke enthusiastically about joining the New York Colored Troops. These conversations usually ended with his promise to Eamon to remain on the farm. As time passed, however, and Reese read accounts of the heroism in combat by colored companies, he spoke of his desire to join up.

Eamon listened quietly as Reese spoke and then said, "Reese, I see you are wantin' to go and fight and I do admire your courage. But it is enough that our Sean is doin' just that."

"But I feel I want to be there, too, where it's all happenin'—to fight for freedom . . ."

Eamon tried to assure him. "Reese, there is no need for you to go. Your work here on the farm is just as important, us growin' and supplyin' food for the brave lads."

Often after such conversations, they would finish their chores in silence until Eamon signaled the return to the house where Maureen awaited with a fine cooked meal.

The McCullough's were aware of Reese's increasing despondency and dreaded the possibility of losing him. On many occasions, as they lay awake in the night, they talked about it.

"The boy is sure set on goin', I fear," Eamon said, sadly.

"Well, we had better be findin' another lad to come help with the chores. You cannot do all the work yourself, husband."

Eamon sighed. "It will not be the same. Reese is family. I trust him with my life. But, I suppose you are right, darlin'. I hafta think about replacin' him while he is gone . . . if he does go . . . oh, Jaysus, I hope to God he does not!"

*   *   *

In July 1864, Sean received two letters: one from Jessica; the other, from his parents. He crept over to a corner of the compound to be alone. With anxious fingers, he tore open Jessica's letter.

June 5, 1864

My dearest,

How I worry for you and long for you. I pray for you every day and cry for you every night. Dear heart, when will we see each other again? I cannot bear the separation. Are you eating enough? Are you sleeping enough? Are you well? Please take care of yourself. Be strong, my darling. I have heard terrible things about Andersonville. My heart breaks for you and I anguish over the thought of any pain you may be suffering. I pray to God I will see you soon.

I close with good wishes from mother and father and love, love, love,

From your devoted Jessica

Her tearful entreaties broke Sean's heart. He felt like shouting out against the sorrow. Over and over again, he kissed the letter and whispered her name. After a while, he opened the mail from home. When he finished reading, he put the sheet of paper down. A sound of pain escaped his lips. He closed his eyes and shook his head. Oh, my God, Reese . . . Reese . . . ! He picked up the letter and reread the words:

June 10, 1864

Dear Son,

In January, Reese went off to fight with the colored troops. His regiment was in the Battle of Olustee in Florida. It must have been terrible, so many casualties. Reese, poor boy, was mortally wounded. The government says they are sending us his medal for outstanding bravery since we are his only "family".

The poor lad gave his life. We are mournin' his death somethin' awful. We tried to stop him but he was so determined—the good Lord rest his soul.

Do not worry about us and the farm. We hired a strong,
young lad to help with the planting and fertilizing and he
will stay with us through the harvesting, as well.

The Lord bless you and keep you safe.

Your loving Da

Sean pressed both letters hard to his chest. He sat alone for a long while, listening to the prayers of the sick and dying who lay half-naked and covered with vermin and filth. Hot tears coursed down his face. How much suffering must one endure in a lifetime? How can one heart break into so many pieces?

At that moment, Lt. Abrams approached. Sean welcomed his company—someone to speak with. He liked the lieutenant and was grateful for his help. Sean told him about the news from home. They chatted for quite a while: the earnest young officer consoled the young sergeant as best he could and then left him to his own thoughts.

Sean wondered about Reese's last moments. "I pray they were swift," he whispered hoarsely. He closed his eyes and recited: "The Lord is my shepherd; I shall not want . . . Yea, though I walk through the valley of the shadow of death, I will fear no evil . . ." As tears fell, he could see Reese's wide smile and hear the echoes of his laughter.

*   *   *

The 54th Massachusetts Infantry Regiment, one of the first black units, had fought valiantly at the Battle of Olustee, in Florida, on the 20th of February 1864. Fifty-five hundred Union soldiers with 16 cannon opposed the Confederates, who almost equaled them in number. They faced each other in open forest and Reese's unit "fought like devils" in one of the bloodiest battles that took the lives of 1861 Union soldiers and 946 Confederates.

CHAPTER XX

*O*N NOVEMBER 8, 1864, Abraham Lincoln was reelected 17ᵗʰ President of the Union. On March 4, 1865, after weeks of rain, thousands of people stood in water and mud on Pennsylvania Avenue, around the grounds of the Capitol, to listen to his second inaugural address.

"Fellow-Countrymen," he said, " . . . there is less occasion for an extended address than there was at the first." He mentioned that in his first inaugural address while he spoke of saving the Union without war, there were many who were seeking to destroy it without war. "Both parties deprecated war, but one of them would rather make war than let the nation survive, and the other would accept war rather than let it perish, and the war came."

He ended with an intensity that moved all who listened. "With malice toward none, with charity for all . . . let us strive to finish the work we are in . . . to do all which may achieve and cherish a just and lasting peace . . . among ourselves and with all nations."

In a little more than a month, President Lincoln lay mortally wounded, shot by John Wilkes Booth, at the Ford Theater in Washington, D.C. Just five days before, General Lee and his Army had surrendered at the Appomattox Court House in Virginia.

As the war moved inexorably to its end, the death toll in Andersonville multiplied to such proportions that by April of 1865, more than 12,000 Union prisoners were buried, shoulder to shoulder, in shallow graves—each identified by a small, numbered marker—in desolate, barren land near the prison complex. Sean often participated in laying these fallen comrades to rest. Hardened by living with death for so long, he barely uttered a word or shed a tear; only his eyes reflected the deep pain; only his heart asked, where are our green flags now?

With the War ended, released prisoners were being shipped to the parole camp near Vicksburg, Mississippi, a repatriation center, where they boarded Mississippi river boats to be transported North. One such side-wheeled river steamer was the SULTANA, capable of carrying 376 passengers. On April 21, 1865, it left New Orleans, Louisiana, for Vicksburg with 100 cabin passengers, a cargo of sugar and livestock. When it made its regular stop there, the engineer discovered the boilers were leaking dangerously. A quick repair job was done. Meanwhile, waiting released prisoners, Sean among them, swarmed onto the decks so rapidly that the usual muster roles were not taken. Soon there were more than 2,000 soldiers crowding every inch of the overburdened ship.

The Mississippi was at flood stage and the strong currents were of deep concern to the ship's Capt. Mason. On the 26th, they docked at Memphis, Tennessee, where some soldiers disembarked and the cargo of sugar was unloaded. The ship was detained while another leaky boiler was repaired. Finally, the SULTANA departed, leaving behind those who had gone ashore and had not returned by sailing time. The overloaded ship now labored toward Cairo, Illinois, where most of the servicemen were to disembark.

Everything appeared to be in order as the steamer went puffing upstream against a stronger than usual current. Sean could hardly wait to dock and head for home. He pictured his reunion with his beloved Jessica and his parents a thousand times in his mind. As he sat lost in reverie, he suddenly became aware of Capt. Mason's voice, confiding to his first mate, " . . . and there are six times more passengers than she usually carries. Listen to how the big paddle wheels are straining and thrashing in the high waters. That's a mighty strong current!"

Sean's heart sank. Oh, please God, don't let anything go wrong!

We are only a few hours away. Just a few more miles to Cairo. He silently recited the Lord's Prayer.

The SULTANA continued to make progress, though slowly. Then at 2 o'clock, in the morning of April 27th, it happened. When the ship passed a group of islands known as the Hens and Chickens, the weakened, leaky boilers exploded with a gush of steam that filled the night air, hissing and sputtering, and with a crash that could be heard in Memphis. A pillar of fire lit the sky and could be seen for miles around.

Nearby ships raced against the engorged water in an attempt to give assistance, but the SULTANA was disintegrating. Bodies, machinery, wood planks and railings—everything on board went hurtling into the murky river. Fire exploded in some sections of the ship. Many jumped rather than face the inferno. Hundreds of wounded were unable to keep afloat and disappeared into the turbulence of the dark waters.

Sean, in the bow of the ship, along with others, threw pieces of wood and debris overboard to the struggling victims who were praying, cursing, crying for help. Their bodies bobbed like so many corks. The flames had not reached the bow of the ship but when the fire changed direction, it became a further threat. Men, too weak to swim, threw themselves into the water rather than face the flames.

The SULTANA finally ran aground on a small island where Sean set his men to foraging. They were able to construct a crude raft upon which more than twenty men scrambled, as others clung to its rough edges. Luckily, one of the rescue boats found them drifting downstream in the direction of Memphis.

More than 1700 perished in this disaster, but overshadowed by the events of the day, it did not receive the attention that a calamity of such proportions deserved. The President had been murdered just eleven days before, a new President—Andrew Johnson—was in the White House, the War was over and the nation now turned to finding closure in reconstruction.

An official inquiry produced voluminous documentation that resulted in nothing. One of the worst sea tragedies was barely noted. The true horror of it all would be described by survivors when they returned home.

The McCullough's had not heard from or anything about Sean for many months. There was talk and they read newspaper reports about the release of prisoners of war. They heard briefly about the riverboat SULTANA capsizing, but did not, for a moment, suspect that this event would impact their lives.

Maureen and Eamon spent tortured days and nights wondering, praying for Sean's return, all the while frozen with fear each time someone unfamiliar approached the house. The delivery of that official letter about Reese was painfully fresh in their memory.

One day, a uniformed fellow on horseback came to a halt on their path. When Eamon stepped out the front door, the soldier asked, "Would you be the McCullough's?"

"I am Eamon McCullough and who might you be?" His voice trembled.

"I am Sgt. John Riley, sir. I have a letter for you from Lt. Joshua Abrams who I served with in the War."

Eamon rubbed his sweaty hands down the front of his overalls. Why was the lieutenant writing to them? He reached for the letter from the stranger's outstretched hand. The envelope was stained and wrinkled. "I thank you kindly. Can I offer you somethin' to eat or drink? You look tired."

Sgt. Riley smiled. "I would be most grateful to you, sir. Been ridin' a couple of days with hardly any sleep . . . just anxious to do the lieutenant's bidding and get home to my family."

An anxious Maureen, peering through the curtains the whole time, bit her lip as she observed the soldier handing Eamon something—was it a letter? Oh, Lord! For a moment, she could barely breathe.

At last, they came into the house. Eamon asked, "Darlin', would you get Sgt. Riley somethin' to eat. He has traveled for days with this letter for us and is worn out." He turned to the sergeant,

"Excuse me while I read this. Perhaps it is news about my son." Nervous fingers tore at the envelope.

30 April 1865

Dear Mr. and Mrs. McCullough,

First let me say that Sean is safe, that he is in hospital in Memphis recovering from his ordeal on the Sultana. Good fortune allowed him and some men to escape the scene of the disaster and, mercifully, he was rescued. The men were so weak, so feverish, that they were taken immediately for treatment.

I, too, was on the Sultana, but lost track of Sean while helping one of the two women on board. I did not see Sean again until, unexpectedly, I found him in the hospital. Providence must have led me to him. We could not believe our eyes and thanked God for our deliverance from peril.

Sean asked me to get word to you as soon as possible. It should not be too long before he is strong enough to make his way home. Knowing how courageous he is, I am sure you will see your boy again shortly.

Your Sincere Servant,

Lt. Joshua Abrams

The sergeant sat at the kitchen table enjoying hot soup and homemade biscuits, while Maureen watched her husband reading the letter. She did not want to be rude in front of the stranger but she grew impatient as Eamon read silently. When her husband burst into uncontrollable tears, she expected the worst. "Eamon, what is it? Have we lost our boy?"

"Oh, no, my darlin'," he was quick to assure her. "He is all right . . . in a hospital, just weak, that is all. He will be home soon, luv. We will have our Sean again." He threw his arms around his weeping wife.

"Thank you, Blessed Virgin. Thank you Sweet Jesus," she breathed.

The sergeant shared their joy. He wiped away a tear quietly making its way down his cheek.

Later, when the sergeant went out to prepare his horse and saddle up, Eamon remarked. "This is the very same officer Sean wrote us about. You know, the one of Jewish faith that gave him a blanket and his own medicine when our boy was sufferin' . . ."

"Oh, yes, you are right. Sean said he did believe that the officer saved his life. The good Lord bless him."

"Wifey, dear, do you recall what you promised the Lord if our son survived the terrible times he was goin' through?"

"What are you sayin', Eamon?"

"Now, do not be gettin' angry, but you did say if Sean comes home to us, you would let him do anythin' that would make him happy."

"And what is that supposed to mean, husband?"

"Well, I am thinkin', that means Sean can marry the girl he loves."

"Startin' that again, are you?" Maureen's voice rose.

"Just remindin' you of the promise you made the Lord."

"Husband, let me be or 'tis an Irish hoist I will be givin' you." She flashed him a look that made it clear that the conversation was over.

Eamon concluded that she must be very angry if she threatened to give him a kick in the arse!

When Sgt. Riley was ready to leave, he had asked Eamon if he knew how he could get to the Wahlberg farm. "I have another letter to deliver to a Miss Jessica Wahlberg. The lieutenant said you would know where they live."

"That we do, lad. Let us go out front and I will show you the way." Eamon noticed the look of chagrin on Maureen's face as he turned toward the door. "I will be back in a few minutes, luv."

A downcast Maureen sat at the table. She was thankful that

Sean had been spared but she dreaded what might be in store. When Eamon returned, he saw his wife wiping away tears. "Oh, Eamon," she whimpered, "the good Lord gave me back my son only to lose him again."

"Darlin', what are you sayin' . . . losin' your boy. What nonsense!"

"Nonsense, you say! My son is goin' to marry out of the Church! How can you live with that?"

"Now, now. We do not know what Sean is goin' to do, do we?" Let the boy come home and let us be thankful. There is time to deal with the rest later." He kissed her on the forehead and held her close. A promise to the Lord is a promise to be kept, but I will not be remindin' her of that again, at least, not for a while.

*　　*　　*

Sgt. Riley found the Wahlberg farm easily. He was invited in when he introduced himself and explained his mission. Jessica screamed with joy when he handed her the letter. She was sure it was good news. As she ran across the room to read it in private, the Wahlberg's exchanged nervous glances. Betty led the sergeant to the kitchen where she insisted he have a cup of tea and a slice of her "delicious, homemade chocolate cake". Morris joined them at the table and chatted with the soldier.

Soon, Jessica, all aglow and breathless, came running with the news. "Sean is coming home. He is all right! Oh, Mama and Papa, I am so happy. Please be happy for me!" She hugged the letter to her breast. Her parents could not help but feel her joy but they also felt deep concern for her future. Betty's eyes lifted heavenward, as Morris patted her hand.

Jessica read and reread the letter which described Sean's rescue and told her how much Sean loved her. Every few minutes, she emitted squeals of pleasure. Evidently, Lt. Abrams had written the letter exactly as Sean had dictated it.

Her parents were anxious to know what the letter contained but did not want to question her in front of the sergeant, lest it embarrass her. Morris told his wife, "She will read it to us in due time." Betty pressed a hand to her bosom and sighed.

The sergeant was oblivious to it all—lost in the smooth, moist sweetness of the best chocolate cake he had ever tasted.

CHAPTER XXI

TEN DAYS PASSED since Sgt. Riley's visit, days through which the McCullough's waited eagerly for Sean's return. On the morning of the eleventh day, when Eamon was ploughing the field, he saw a gaunt figure approach the farmhouse. His eyes squinted in the bright sunlight as he tried to focus them. "Oh, Jaysus, can it be? 'Tis!" he shouted. He ran toward the house, calling, "Sean, son, is it really you?" Father and son embraced, holding back tears.

Maureen came running to the door. Exclamations of joy mingled with sobs. "Oh, my darlin' boy. Home at last you are. Bless the Lord. How I have prayed for this moment." Her heart hurt as she observed how frail he looked, his cheeks hollowed from malnutrition and starvation. She mustered all her strength to remain controlled. Putting her arm around Sean's shoulders, she said, "Come now and let us have a bite to eat." She tenderly stroked his hair, trying hard to smile with lips that trembled.

Eamon found it difficult to hide his feelings, especially as he watched Maureen plainly struggling with hers.

As they sat around the kitchen table enjoying a hearty Irish stew and freshly baked soda bread, Sean could not refrain from emitting gastronomical sounds of pleasure. "Mam, how I have longed for your cookin'!" He voraciously consumed the generous portions set before him.

After a while, Sean spoke of his escape and miraculous rescue from the Sultana and of Lt. Abrams. "I owe my life to that man. If not for him, I would be lyin' side by side with the dead boys at Andersonville." A gagging sound escaped his throat.

"Sean, darlin', let us not speak of these things now. You need to rest. Thank the Lord, you are home, safe." Maureen bent over to kiss him on the forehead.

"Mam is right, son. It is time to go on with your life. A few more home cooked meals and you will be as good as new," Eamon added.

"I suppose so, Da, but it will be hard to forget the men who fought with me—brave boys willin' to die for the Union—and I will never forget who it was that kept *me* from dyin' . . . and, just as much, my love for Jessica that gave me strength and determination to stay alive." Seeing his mother wince, Sean added hastily, "And, of course, you Mam and Da, your love has always made me strong."

There was a brief silence. Suddenly, Sean announced, "I am goin' over to the Wahlberg's to visit with them for awhile."

Noticing that his wife was about to speak and afraid of what she might say, Eamon quickly interjected, "That is a grand thing to do, son. They will be happy to see you are home." Maureen shot him one of her withering glances.

The door closed behind Sean. They heard the horse and wagon being led down the path.

There was much rejoicing at the Wahlberg's. They truly loved Sean and were happy that he had survived the Great War. Betty felt her heart would break when she witnessed the passionate longing on her daughter's face as she held Sean, unashamedly, fast in her arms and the way Sean closed his eyes as every fiber of his being quivered with emotion.

They sat together enjoying Betty's delicious cake and making conversation about Sean's experiences. Finally, Jessica said, "Mama, Papa, we would like to go out for a little while. Please? We have so much to talk about. Sean will bring me home before dark."

"Go, my child," Morris told her. "Be careful on the road. We will wait supper for you. Sean, you are welcome to join us."

"Thank you kindly, Mr. Wahlberg, but I promised to return home to eat with my family. I just had to come over to see Jessica and both of you to tell you I am safe."

"You are a good boy, Sean." Betty smiled even though she knew that decisions would soon be made. She loved them both—two beautiful, wonderful children. Oh, God, why must there be problems? She and Morris had had a long talk about the relationship between Jessica and Sean. They were concerned about their daughter's future but had resolved that if compromises were necessary, they were ready to make them. "Meanwhile," Betty had rationalized, "nothing has been decided. Maybe the children will just remain good friends. We'll see." Now, however, observing their glowing faces filled with happiness and anticipation, Betty put her "good friends" theory on the back burner. She watched through the window as the wagon disappeared from view. "Oy vey," she whispered.

*   *   *

Sean and Jessica drove to their favorite trysting place in the woods. "It hasn't changed much, has it?" Sean commented.

"No, darling. I come here almost every day and pour my heart out to you through my poems. I have dozens of them and someday you shall read them all."

Sean looked at her sweet face. She was still the naïve, innocent girl he had fallen in love with and dreamt about while he was away. "I will never leave you again," he promised. He cupped his hand under her chin and gazed deeply into her eyes. Kissing her on the forehead, the tip of her nose, and on her lips, he whispered hoarsely, "Jessica, my beloved, will you be my wife? Will you spend the rest of your life with me, forever and ever? I love you so!"

"Oh, Sean, yes, yes . . . forever and ever! I love you with every ounce of my being."

The sweet fragrance of the surrounding foliage was intoxicating. Deep hues of the dying day created playful shadows around them. Canopies of tree branches welcomed them back. Sean took Jessica into his arms and lifted her out of the wagon. They walked to the place where they had first consummated their love. He looked at her. There was no need to ask. Eyes bespoke desire.

Sean carefully put her down upon the crisp leaves and placed himself upon her, their bodies instantly responding. Slowly, gently, they relished every moment. Tears mingled with fervent kisses and sweet promises.

"Jessica, my love, every minute away from you was agony. I thought of you even in battle. It gave me the will to stay alive. All I could think about was comin' home to you . . . to hold you again . . . to love you again. Now, at last!"

"Sean, dearest, don't say another word. Just hold me close to your heart."

They stayed there in each other's arms until shadows lengthened as the sun's rays slowly disappeared from view. It was dusk. Sean brought Jessica home. When he walked her to the door, the Wahlberg's could not help but notice how flushed he looked and how their daughter glowed.

Jessica ran up the stairs, calling to her parents, "I'll wash for supper and be right down."

A jubilant Sean jumped up into the wagon and waved to the Wahlberg's as he started for home.

Betty turned to Morris. There was no need for words.

CHAPTER XXII

THE HOMESTEAD ACT was in effect since January 1, 1863. Two hundred and seventy million acres of public domain were turned over to private citizens. The Act provided that at the end of five years, after the homesteader was "proving up"—building a home and commencing farming—he was granted a patent to his 160 acres.

The lure of the timberlands, the discovery of gold, and suitable farm land attracted hordes of immigrants. With the end of the Civil War, many veterans turned their eyes Westward.

The McCullough's sat, enjoying their evening meal. They listened with interest as Sean spoke about the Homestead Act. "A man can carve out a wonderful livin' with 160 acres and make a fortune for his family. All you have to do is pay a filin' fee of $18, and not all at once, either."

As he spoke, Maureen became more and more uneasy. Finally, she blurted out, "Are you thinkin' of goin' out there? You have just come home. Oh, Sweet Jesus, the danger of it all! Indians killin' and scalpin'! All them rivers to cross and mountains . . ."

"Mam, I have been 'to see the elephant'—I have lived through a bad experience. After seein' Union boys and Confederates killin' each other, the lootin' and burnin' of cities . . ." He inhaled deeply. "Nothing can be as bad as all that. Anyway, treaties have been signed with some of the tribes. It is much safer to travel now. There are many Army units patrolling the trail, protecting wagon trains, if necessary. In fact, the government recommends using the Overland Trail as the best route to the West."

"But, son, you are home a short while," Maureen pleaded. "Please do not be leavin' us again."

Eamon swallowed hard. He looked at his son questioningly, at a loss for words.

Sean's heart was heavy. He realized how difficult it must have been for them these past years. Now he would break their hearts again. "Mam, Da, a week ago, Jessica and I were married before a Justice of the Peace in Manhattan, the day we went into the City on the pretense of seeing a popular vaudeville show."

Maureen had remained relatively silent of late concerning the time Sean spent with Jessica. Eamon convinced her that it would be the best way to handle the situation. Secretly, he hoped his wife would come to accept the inevitable.

As Sean continued to speak, attempting to console them, Maureen alternated between wringing her hands and clutching the cross at her throat. Furious, she shouted, "So now it's the two of you together who will be leavin' to live in sin!" She spat out the words.

"Dammit, Mam!"

Maureen recoiled. She had never heard her son use strong language.

"Jessica is my wife!"

Lowering his voice, Sean continued, "We knew you would not give us your blessings, so Jessica and I made a decision. We took our vows before a Justice of the Peace."

"Your vows!" Maureen shrieked. "What about your vows to the Church? How could you defy us like that? Marryin' out of our faith . . . bad luck will surely follow you. Lord, have mercy!"

Eamon tried to calm her. "Now, now, darlin', there is nothin' good can come of this hollerin' and bickerin'. Remember your promise, if the Good Lord brought Sean back to us. Think of what we went through because I was a Protestant. We worked things out and we have been just fine."

She was not to be pacified. "Why did I listen to you, husband?

Do not say anythin', you told me. Just be quiet and let things work themselves out, you said. Well, look at how things worked out! I have a heathen for a son!" She stormed out of the kitchen. The bedroom door slammed.

Sean turned to his father. "What can I do? I have loved Jessica since the first time I saw her when Reese and I rescued her father from their overturned wagon. I carried that love in my heart all through the battles in fields of blood, all through the sufferin' in Andersonville—always thinkin' of comin' home to Jessica and sharin' my life with her. I love you and Mam and don't want to cause you hurt, but, Da, don't I deserve to find happiness after all I have been through? It breaks my heart that Mam will not give us her blessing."

"Son, it is a hard thing for her to accept right now but I am sure she will come 'round. She truly loves you. Tell me, do the Wahlberg's know about your gettin' married and all?"

"Yes, Da. It was difficult for them, too, but they put their daughter's happiness above their feelin's."

"Well, Sean, Jessica is not the colleen I had in mind, but she is a fine girl. I wish the best for both of you but . . . do you have to leave us?"

"Da, listen to me. There's a whole new world out there waitin' for folks like us. Just think of the opportunities. A quarter of a square mile of government surveyed land waitin' for anyone 21 years of age or older and head of household. All I need is the filin' fee and I have much more than that from the money I sent home while I was in the War. Right, Da?"

"Sure and we put all that aside for you but, Sean, goin' so far away from us . . . I cannot help bein' fearful. It is an ambitious undertakin' . . . a dangerous one . . ."

"Da, there's a future to be had in the West."

"You know, son, there are lots of opportunities here in New York. I can take you down to Tammany. They are always lookin' for educated young men to work for the Party."

"Da, I'm not interested in getting' involved with Tammany. I don't have a leanin' toward politics. If President Lincoln was still with us, I might have considered working with the government, but . . ."

"Sean, how about takin' a ride with me into the City, anyway. I would like to see the boys downtown and introduce you around. It has been a long time."

Although recognizing the ploy, Sean decided to humor his father. He deserved at least that much. "All right, Da, we can do that."

"Thanks, son." Eamon enjoyed a sense of satisfaction. He was sure an opportunity would present itself that would convince Sean that his future was right here at home. "Well, goodnight, Sean. See you bright and early in the mornin'. Get some rest." He kissed him on the forehead.

"Goodnight, Da. I love you."

Eamon embraced him and hurried away to tell Maureen about his plan. He hoped it would assuage her. That night, he prayed for another miracle. The Lord had brought his son home from the War and now he fervently asked that his son remain near him and Maureen.

Eamon had maintained minimal contact with Tammany through the War years, except for an occasional stop to say hello to whomever he ran into. The same secretary at the front desk always greeted him warmly, as he did now. "Good to see you Mr. McCullough and surely this must be your boy Sean, all grown up."

"Yes, and he is just back from the War, thank the Lord."

"That's wonderful. What can we do for you?"

"Well, I thought we could see Mr. Tweed about a job here for my son . . ."

"Mr. Tweed is a busy man. I'd have to arrange for an interview."

"We would surely appreciate that."

Just then, the door opened and a bearded, pompous man, with an entourage trailing behind, hastened across the anteroom toward the door through which the McCullough's had originally gone to meet Big Tim Kelly, a lifetime ago.

Eamon mustered his courage and called out, "Sir, Mr. Tweed, could we have a word?"

"Boss" Tweed stopped in his tracks, turning to look at the audacious fellow before him. He was amused. Not too many people would have the guts to address him this way. A couple of his men stepped forward but Tweed signaled them to desist. "Who might you be and what is it you want with me?"

Eamon extended his hand. "I am Eamon McCullough and this is my son Sean, a veteran of the War, a good Union soldier of the Irish Brigade, and I would like to talk to you about the possibility of a job for him."

The secretary hastily interrupted, "Mr. McCullough, I told you we had to set up an appointment!"

Sean, embarrassed, was about to urge his father to leave.

Tweed laughed. "That's all right. I like this man's style. Come into my office, you two, and let's talk."

The secretary soon returned with a piece of paper in hand which he handed to Tweed, who quickly scanned it. "Mr. McCullough, I see that you were a ward heeler in the Sixth before you moved uptown, a good committeeman. There's always a place for loyalty and always a place for a bright lad in the organization. I'm sure he will be a good team worker like his father was. The apple doesn't fall far from the tree, eh?" He laughed and winked broadly at Eamon.

Tweed stood up, indicating the meeting was over. "Make an appointment to see me one day next week. I'd like to talk to the boy about a job in the accounting department." He shook hands with Eamon and gave Sean a resounding pat on the back. "You'll do just fine, my boy. We look out for each other here. Just like one big family." He laughed again.

On the way out, the secretary informed them that they were to return on Friday of the next week, at 1 p.m. Both McCullough's thanked him and left.

When they returned to the farm, Eamon described their meeting to an anxious Maureen. He was so proud as he told her about their conversation. Maureen turned to Sean, "Son, this is an honor indeed, such an important man givin' you his personal attention. I hope you are thinkin' of seein' the man next week."

Sean looked at her. He wished he could lift that veil of anxiety that clouded her words and actions since he told her about the marriage. "You are right, Mam, but with all due respect, I'll decide that after I talk it over with Jessica."

Maureen flinched. "So it is her decision, is it?"

Eamon quickly interceded. "Now, darlin', he is married and it is only proper that he discuss it with his wife . . . like I have always done with you when decisions were to be made."

Sean cut the conversation short by announcing, "I'm goin' over to the Wahlberg's. Da, I'll be here early in the mornin' to help with the chores."

Eamon glanced at Maureen. It was going to be a rough night.

When Sean told Jessica about the job offer, she was excited by the prospect of his working in the City and, possibly, of their living in Manhattan. "Oh, Sean, life will be so different! We could rent a flat and I could get a job as a saleslady or even a secretary. It all sounds so thrilling!"

"Sweetheart, I'll keep my appointment with Mr. Tweed if you are sure you want me to do this. Remember, we had all those plans to go on a wondrous adventure to the West."

"Yes, my dear, I know, but our parents would be so happy if we changed those plans. They really want desperately for us to stay. We can be happy anywhere, darling. At least, give it a try. You are so smart, Sean, I'm sure you will go far in Tammany Hall. You might be mayor someday!" She giggled and hugged him.

"We'll see, my beloved, we'll see." He drew her closer and kissed her passionately.

CHAPTER XXIII

E AMON DROVE SEAN into the City for his appointment at Tammany Hall. He dropped him off and promised to return in a couple of hours, after he made his deliveries.

The secretary showed Sean into Tweed's chambers. After exchanging amenities, Tweed launched into a sales pitch about the position he had in mind for Sean, in the accounting department. "You'll be earning $1,200 per year plus employee benefits. This is a marvelous opportunity for a bright young man such as the likes of you. There will also be an extra bonus at Christmas because you served your country in the Great War."

"Thank you, Mr. Tweed. I hope I live up to your expectations of me." Sean was enthused by what appeared to be an ideal set of circumstances. Maybe life here in the City would be best for him and Jessica. He did owe it to her and his family to give it a chance. "When do I report for work, Sir?"

"Good lad." Tweed shook Sean's hand. "We'll see you at 9 a.m. sharp, on Monday."

An optimistic Sean found Eamon already waiting outside. When he told his father the good news, he was overjoyed. "Oh, thank the Lord. I am so happy, Sean. I can hardly wait to tell your mother. This will be the answer to her prayers."

"Not altogether, Da."

"Well, we will work on that. I am positive she will come 'round."

Sean began to feel better about things.

After one week at Tammany Hall, Sean realized that the Tweed Ring's construction projects were riddled with bribes and inflated contracts. Sean was soon aware that rumors he heard were true. "Boss" Tweed was lining his pockets and those of his friends and family with huge sums of money he received as kickbacks.

He came home incensed by what he had discovered. Over supper, he told his parents, "Mam, Da, I have resigned from my job. Please listen before you say anything." Maureen and Eamon both reacted with loud exclamations of disbelief. Sean continued, "Tammany Hall is all about politics and money. Sure, the unions are good for their members and Tweed created a lot of work programs—lots of jobs—but the power is in the hands of a small group of greedy men, stealing from the City government." He provided more details about the inflated contracts and the graft— how Tweed and his cronies take advantage of their positions to obtain large sums of money and property. He concluded with, "I'm sorry it didn't work out. I want no part of that den of robbers!"

*   *   *

Political corruption had long been characteristic of Tammany Hall. By 1865, now under the reign of William Marcy "Boss" Tweed and his three "bedfellows": Pete Sweeney, Richard Connolly and Oakley Hall, fraudulent deals reached their highest proportions.

William Marcy Tweed was born in New York City on April 3, 1823. He attended public school and learned the trade of chair making. As an adult, he had such jobs as chair maker, bookkeeper, and volunteer fireman. In 1851, he became an alderman to New York City. In 1852, he was elected to the House of Representatives; in 1856, the New York City Board of Advisors; and, in 1868, to the New York Senate. Ambitious, he quickly rose through the ranks, building a political machine by placing friends in jobs. By 1863, he was the head of the New York City political machine.

Tweed had tremendous public support because of the major work projects and charities he sponsored. New buildings, streets, parks, docks, sewers were all promoted by spending tax funds—construction contracts for which were highly inflated. The poor and working class immigrants strongly supported him. He found them jobs and helped them find their relatives. Those who were arrested for petty crimes were usually bailed out or released after a bribe in the judge's chambers. At Christmas, ward captains delivered turkeys to the indigent, helped with family celebrations and with funerals, and, at election time, reminded the recipients who their friends were.

Defrauding the City government provided Tweed and his cohorts with a lifestyle that far superseded their salaries. Tweed had a mansion on Fifth Avenue and an estate in Greenwich, Conn. All on a salary of $2,500 a year!

Thomas Nast, a famous cartoonist for Harper's Weekly and the New York Times, launched an unrelenting series of attacks on William Tweed and Tammany Hall. The questions raised by the Times eventually exposed Tammany's scandal-racked activities.

By 1870, Tweed was convicted and sentenced to 12 years in prison for defrauding the City of millions of dollars. He escaped to Spain, was recognized from a Nast cartoon and returned to jail in New York, where he died several years later.

*   *   *

The McCullough household was filled with tension after Sean's announcement that he had quit his job at Tammany. Conversations were stilted. Talk of going West resurged when Eamon and Sean conversed. Maureen, her hopes shattered, barely spoke to her son. Every evening, Sean would take leave of his parents to go to the Wahlberg's.

Betty would always ask, "How are your parents, Sean? You know, we would like to get together with them. We should be celebrating. After all, we are family."

"Mrs. Wahlberg, I think for the time bein' we had better leave things alone."

This evening, however, when Betty dropped the subject, Morris was not inclined to do so. "Betty, tomorrow we are going over to see Maureen and Eamon to have a talk. After all, as you said, we are now family. Sean, please tell your mama and papa that we will be coming by tomorrow evening, yes?"

Sean was grateful that someone was taking the initiative. "I will tell them in the morning. I too am anxious for all of us to have a talk. To tell the truth, my father is not a problem anymore, but my mother is a different story. You have to understand, she is a deeply religious woman—a devout Catholic. She feels that I have deserted the Church and turned against her and everything she brought me up to believe in . . . and add to that our plans to go West . . ."

Jessica began to cry. "Will your mother ever accept me?"

Sean rushed to her side. "Please, please, Jessica. I didn't mean to upset you."

Betty, too, began to cry. Morris threw his hands up in the air. "*Gott in himmel!*" Everybody, please, calm down." He embraced his wife. "Sh-h-h-h, darling, we will work things out. Do not cry. Please."

When Sean broke the news, at breakfast, about the proposed visit, Eamon agreed. "That is just fine. It will be good to talk things over. It has been long enough."

Maureen lashed out. "I have nothin' to say to them. Their daughter has bewitched my son and he has turned his back on the Lord."

"Now, Maureen, my dear, try to be reasonable. Open your heart to your precious son and his lovely wife. Jesus taught us to love one another and to turn the other cheek. It is time for you to do that. Think of your son's happiness—he has endured enough sorrow these past few years."

"And what is he doin' now? Turnin' against his faith and leavin' his mam to go off to some strange place full of heathens!"

Sean stiffened. He resented his mother's harsh comments. "Mam, aren't you happy that I am alive, that I am saved?"

"Saved? You will not be saved, marryin' out of the Church!"

"I am truly sorry to cause you grief, Mam, but . . ."

Maureen sobbed. "All my life it seems I cannot have a bit of happiness but that it is taken right away from me."

Eamon tried to embrace her. She pulled away. "Husband, leave me be. 'Tis only bad advice you are good for!"

Sean begged, "Mam, Da, please! I can't bear to see you like this. I am truly sad, Mam, that you cannot open your heart to us. I suppose leavin' *is* the only choice for me and Jessica." He threw his arms up in the air in a helpless gesture and walked out of the kitchen.

Eamon spent most of the day with his tearful wife trying to convince her that Sean was entitled to make decisions about his life, that she should be thankful he was spared. By evening all he could hope for was that she would receive the Wahlberg's graciously, at least, for Sean's sake.

When Jessica and her parents arrived at the front door with Sean, Eamon had to hold onto Maureen who looked like she was about to dash away. He hoped his wife would remember the friendly relationship they had always enjoyed with the Wahlberg's.

Eamon greeted them. "Come in, come in. It is good to see you." He shook Morris' hand.

Maureen stood frozen as Betty tried to embrace her. "Darling, we must talk together about our children and their future. My dear, it is time for celebration. Our children are married!"

Maureen flinched. Eamon looked pleadingly at his wife. She opened her mouth as though to speak, but did not. He quickly suggested, "Luv, how about servin' up some of them wonderful biscuits you made? That would be fine with a good cup of tea. I am sure Betty and Morris would enjoy that."

"Oh, yes, that would be lovely, Maureen," Betty said.

Sean held Jessica's hand. When Maureen turned toward the kitchen, Jessica ran to her. "Please, let me help you, Mrs. McCull . . ."

"Thank you, no need to." Maureen moved away.

Sean reached for Jessica, feeling her hurt.

"Let us go into the parlor," Eamon suggested. "Make yourselves comfortable. Sean, you go see if Mam needs some help." His look was meaningful.

Sean found his mother standing near the sink, tears streaming down her face. He wrapped his arms around her. "Oh, Mam, I do love you so. Please don't be angry. I want so much for you to be happy for us."

"You have broken my heart. It is too late now to make amends. You married out of your religion and the Church and livin' in sin. How can I accept that? The Wahlberg's are good people but they are not of our faith."

"Mam, that is not important anymore. Jessica and I are truly in love and we are married. Nothing can change that. If we have to, we will make our way alone."

"I know, I know. You have made it clear that you are goin' to leave us—all that talk about the West . . ."

Sean pleaded, "Mam, why can't you bend? The Wahlberg's are willin' to set aside their objections. They're just thinkin' of their daughter's happiness—and mine."

Maureen was silent. She brushed her damp face with the back of her hand, smoothed down the front of her apron, and said, grudgingly, "Well, I will pray to the Lord for guidance. Now, take this tray into the parlor."

For the first time, Sean thought he saw a glimmer of hope.

They sat in the parlor all evening. Eamon and Morris had their usual discussion about the politics of the day. Betty and Maureen exchanged polite conversation about the latest in style for women. The newlyweds sat quietly, holding hands, wondering when "the talk" would begin.

After they finished their refreshments, Morris turned to all of them. "I think it is time that we cleared the air. We must talk about our children and their future. Maureen, I appreciate the fact that you have a problem because of the difference in our religions. But think about it. Your son was in such peril and could have been killed at any given moment in the War, like so many were. But, God brought him home to us. Shouldn't Sean be able to choose how and with whom he wants to continue his life—a life he fought so hard to keep? Maureen, the children love each other. They are married. Perhaps *this* is God's will. Why should we stand in the way?"

*   *   *

The horse and wagon stood on the path in front of the McCullough house. Eamon and Maureen watched as Sean loaded household items, bed linens, and a variety of bottled and boxed foodstuffs.

Jessica and Sean had decided to head West before the fall weather sets in and while the grass on the plains would still be long enough for animals to graze. Sean and his father had worked hard preparing the farm wagon for the journey. Covers, waterproofed with linseed oil, were made for the front and back ends to keep out dust and rain. Eamon fitted the wagon with a well-equipped toolbox, a water barrel, and a set of hardwood brakes.

The Wahlberg's soon arrived, bringing Jessica and her belongings—and, of course, some wonderful cakes which Betty assured them "will give you strength and energy."

At that remark, Maureen quipped, "There's lots of soda bread in them boxes to put muscle on a man."

They smiled at each other. Acceptance had finally brought peace.

When all was in readiness, they hugged and kissed and exchanged words of love, hope for the future, and promises to keep in contact as often as possible. There were no dry eyes.

"The Good Lord bless you and keep you safe," Maureen cried, as the wagon pulled away.

Drawing Jessica to him, Sean mustered his best Gaelic accent. "Oh, darlin', 'tis goin' ta be grand altogether." Their laughter floated back on a warm, summer breeze.